Praise for
Planet of the Apes

"*Planet of the Apes* is tomorrow's version of *Gulliver's Travels*."
— *Louisville Times*

"This novel is respectfully descended from Swift on one side, and Verne on the other."
— *The Atlantic Monthly*

"The tale enables Boulle to dissect, with delicate irony, the stupidity of established authority, the vanity of human ambition, and the nature of our own society. The novel's surprise ending is singularly horrifying."
— *Newark News*

PLANET OF THE APES

Pierre Boulle

Translation by Xan Fielding

A Del Rey® Book

BALLANTINE BOOKS • NEW YORK

A Del Rey® Book
Published by The Random House Publishing Group

Published in the United States by Del Rey Books, an imprint of The Random House Publishing Group, a division of Random House, Inc., New York, and simultaneously in Canada by Random House of Canada Limited, Toronto.

Originally published in French by Editions Rene Julliard, Paris, and in English by Vanguard Press, a division of Random House, Inc., in 1963.

www.delreybooks.com

ISBN 0-345-44798-0

Manufactured in the United States of America

First Ballantine Books Edition: May 2001

OPM 19 18 17 16

ONE

one

Jinn and Phyllis were spending a wonderful holiday, in space, as far away as possible from the inhabited stars.

In those days interplanetary voyages were an everyday occurrence, and interstellar travel not uncommon. Rockets took tourists to the wondrous sites of Sirius, or financiers to the famous stock exchanges of Arcturus and Aldebaran. But Jinn and Phyllis, a wealthy leisured couple, were distinguished in their cosmos for their originality and a few grains of poetry. They wandered over the universe for their pleasure—by sail.

Their ship was a sort of sphere with an envelope—the sail—which was miraculously fine and light and moved through space propelled by the pressure of

light-radiation. Such a machine, left to its own devices in the vicinity of a star (though far enough
away for the field of gravity not to be too powerful), will always move in a straight line in the opposite direction to the star; but since Jinn and Phyllis'
stellar system contained three suns that were relatively close to one another, their vessel received rays
of light along three different axes. Jinn had therefore conceived an extremely ingenious method of
steering. His sail was lined inside with a series of
black blinds that he could roll up or unroll at will,
thus changing the effect of the light-pressure by
modifying the reflecting power of certain sections.
Furthermore, this elastic envelope could be stretched
or contracted as the navigator pleased. Thus, when
Jinn wanted to increase his speed, he gave it the
biggest diameter possible. It would then take the
blasts of radiation on an enormous surface and the
vessel would hurtle through space at a furious ve-
locity, which made his mate Phyllis quite dizzy. He
would also be overcome by vertigo, and they would
then cling passionately to each other, their gaze
fixed on the mysterious and distant depths to which
their flight propelled them. When, on the other
hand, they wanted to slow down, Jinn pressed a
button. The sail would shrink until it became a
sphere just big enough to contain them both,
packed tightly together. The effect of the light became negligible, and this minute bubble, reduced to
nothing more than its own inertia, seemed motion-

less, as though suspended in the void by an invisible thread. The young couple would spend rapturous idle hours in this reduced universe, erected on their own scale and for them alone, which Jinn compared to a becalmed sailing ship and Phyllis to the air bubble of the sea spider.

Jinn knew a number of other tricks, considered as the height of art by sailing cosmonauts: for example, making use of the shadows of the planets and certain satellites in order to change course. He imparted this skill to Phyllis, who was now almost as accomplished as he himself and often more daring. When she held the tiller, she would sometimes fire a broadside that swept them right to the borders of the stellar system, heedless of the resulting magnetic storm, which would start to upset the light-rays and to shake their skiff like a cockleshell. On two or three occasions, waked up with a start by the tempest, Jinn had had quite a struggle snatching the tiller from her and, in order to run for shelter as quickly as possible, starting the auxiliary rocket, which they made it a point of honor never to use except in case of danger.

One day Jim and Phyllis were lying side by side in the middle of their spacecraft without a care in the world, making the most of their holiday by exposing themselves to the rays of their three suns. Eyes closed, Jinn was thinking only of his love for Phyllis. Phyllis lay stretched out on her side, gazing at the immensity of the universe and letting herself be hypnotized, as she often did, by the cosmic sensation of the void.

All of a sudden she came out of her trance, wrinkled her brow, and sat up. An unusual flash of light had streaked across this void. She waited a few seconds and saw a second flash, like a ray being reflected off a shiny object. The cosmic sense she had acquired in the course of these cruises could not deceive her. Moreover, Jinn, when it was pointed out to him, agreed with her, and it was inconceivable that he should make a mistake in this matter: a body sparkling in the light was floating through space, at a distance they could not yet assess. Jinn picked up a pair of binoculars and focused them on the mysterious object, while Phyllis leaned on his shoulder.

"It's not a very big object," he said. "It seems to be made of glass. . . . No, let me look. It's drawing closer. It's going faster than we are. It looks like . . ."

A puzzled expression came into his eyes. He lowered the binoculars, which she at once snatched up.

"It's a bottle, darling."

"A bottle!"

She looked at it, in turn.

"Yes, it's a bottle. I can see it quite clearly. It's made of light-colored glass. It's corked; I can see the seal. There's something white inside that looks like paper—a message, obviously. Jinn, we've got to get hold of it!"

Jinn was of the same opinion and had already

embarked on some skillful maneuvers to place the sphere on the trajectory of the unusual body. He soon succeeded and then reduced his own speed to enable it to catch up with him. Meanwhile Phyllis donned her diving suit and made her way out of the sail by the double trap door. There, holding onto a rope with one hand and brandishing a long-handled scoop in the other, she stood in readiness to retrieve the bottle.

It was not the first time they had come across strange bodies, and the scoop had already been in use. Sailing at low speed, sometimes completely motionless, they had enjoyed surprises and made discoveries that were precluded to travelers by rocket. In her net Phyllis had already gathered up remnants of pulverized planets, fragments of meteorites that had come from the depths of the universe, and pieces of satellites launched at the outset of the conquest of space. She was very proud of her collection; but this was the first time they had come across a bottle, and a bottle containing a message— of that she was certain. She trembled from head to foot with impatience, gesticulating like a spider on the end of its thread as she shouted down the telephone to her companion:

"Slower, Jinn. . . . No, a bit faster than that, it's going to pass us. . . . Starboard. . . . Now hard to port. . . . Hold it. . . . I've got it!"

She gave a triumphant cry and came back inside with her trophy.

It was a largish bottle and its neck had been carefully sealed. A roll of paper could be seen inside.

"Jinn, break it open, hurry up!" Phyllis begged, stamping her foot.

Less impatient, Jinn methodically chipped off the sealing wax. But when the bottle was thus opened, he saw that the paper was stuck fast and could not be shaken out. He therefore yielded to his mate's entreaties and smashed the glass with a hammer. The paper unrolled of its own accord. It consisted of a large number of very thin sheets, covered with tiny handwriting. The message was written in the language of the Earth, which Jinn knew perfectly, having been partly educated on that planet.

An uncomfortable feeling, however, restrained him from starting to read a document that had fallen into their hands in such an inconguous manner; but Phyllis' state of excitement decided him. She was not so well acquainted with the language of the Earth and needed his help.

"Jinn, please!"

He reduced the volume of the sphere so that it floated idly in space, made sure that there was no obstacle in front of them, then lay down beside his companion and began to read the manuscript.

two

I am confiding this manuscript to space, not with the intention of saving myself, but to help, perhaps, to avert the appalling scourge that is menacing the human race. Lord have pity on us! . . .

"The human *race?" Phyllis exclaimed, stressing the second word in her astonishment.*

"That's what it says here," Jinn assured her. "Don't start off by interrupting me." And he went on with his reading.

As for me, Ulysse Mérou, I have set off again with my family in the spaceship. We can keep going for several years. We grow vegetables and fruit on board and have a poultry run. We lack nothing. One day perhaps we shall come across a friendly planet.

This is a hope I hardly dare express. But here, faithfully reported, is the account of my adventure.

It was in the year 2500 that I embarked with two companions in the cosmic ship, with the intention of reaching the region of space where the supergigantic star Betelgeuse reigns supreme.

It was an ambitious project, the most ambitious that had ever been conceived on Earth. Betelgeuse—or Alpha Orionis, as our astronomers called it—is about three hundred light-years distant from our planet. It is remarkable for a number of things. First, its size: its diameter is three or four hundred times greater than that of our sun; in other words, if its center were placed where the sun's center lies, this monster would extend to within the orbit of Mars. Second, its brilliance: it is a star of first magnitude, the brightest in the constellation of Orion, visible on Earth to the naked eye in spite of its distance. Third, the nature of its rays: it emits red and orange lights, creating a most magnificent effect. Finally, it is a heavenly body with a variable glow: its luminosity varies with the seasons, this being caused by the alterations in its diameter. Betelgeuse is a palpitating star.

Why, after the exploration of the solar system, all the planets of which are inhabited, why was such a distant star chosen as the target for the first interstellar flight? It was the learned Professor Antelle who made this decision. The principal organizer of the enterprise, to which he devoted the whole of his enormous fortune, the leader of our expedition, he himself had conceived the spaceship and directed its construction. He told me the reason for his choice during the voyage.

"My dear Ulysse," he said, "it is not much harder, and it would scarcely take any longer, for us to reach Betelgeuse than a much closer star: Proxima Centauris, for example."

At this I saw fit to protest and draw his attention to some recently ascertained astronomical data:

"Scarcely take any longer! But Proxima Centauris is only four light-years away, whereas Betelgeuse . . ."

"Is three hundred, I'm well aware of that. But we shall take scarcely more than two years to reach it, while we should have needed almost as much time to arrive in the region of Proxima Centauris. You don't believe it because you are accustomed to mere flea hops on our planets, for which a powerful acceleration is permissible at the start because it lasts no more than a few minutes, the cruising speed to be reached being ridiculously low and not to be compared with ours. . . . It is time I gave you a few details as to how our ship works.

"Thanks to its perfected rockets, which I had the honor of designing, this craft can move at the highest speed imaginable in the universe for a material body—that is to say, the speed of light minus *epsilon*."

"Minus *epsilon*?"

"I mean it can approach it to within an infinitesimal degree: to within a thousand-millionth, if you care to put it that way."

"Good," I said. "I can understand that."

"What you must also realize is that while we are moving at this speed, our time diverges perceptibly from time on Earth, the divergence being greater the faster we move. At this very moment, since we started this conversation, we have lived several minutes, which correspond to a passage of several months on our planet. At top speed, time will almost stand still for us, but of course we shall not be aware of this. A few seconds for you and me, a few heartbeats, will coincide with a passage of several years on Earth."

"I can understand that, too. In fact, that is the reason why we can hope to reach our destination before dying. But in that case, why a voyage of two years? Why not only a few days or a few hours?"

"I was just coming to that. Quite simply because, to reach the speed at which time almost stands still, with an acceleration acceptable to our organisms, we need about a year. A further year will be necessary to reduce our speed. Now do you understand our flight plan? Twelve months of acceleration; twelve months of reducing speed; between the two, only a few hours, during which we shall cover the main part of the journey. And at the same time you will understand why it scarcely takes any longer to travel to Betelgeuse than to Proxima Centauris.

In the latter case we should have to go through the same indispensable year of acceleration, the same year of deceleration, and perhaps a few minutes instead of a few hours between the two. The overall difference is insignificant. As I'm getting on in years and will probably never be able to make another crossing, I preferred to aim at a distant point straight away, in the hope of finding a world very different from our own."

This sort of conversation occupied our leisure hours on board and at the same time made me appreciate Professor Antelle's prodigious skill all the more. There was no field he had not explored, and I was pleased to have a leader like him on such a hazardous enterprise. As he had foreseen, the voyage lasted about two years of our time, during which three and a half centuries must have elapsed on Earth. That was the only snag about aiming so far into the distance: if we came back one day we should find our planet older by seven or eight hundred years. But we did not care. I even felt that the prospect of escaping from his contemporaries was an added attraction to the professor. He often admitted he was tired of his fellow men. . . .

"Men!" Phyllis again exclaimed.

"Yes, men," Jinn asserted. "That's what it says."

There was no serious incident on the flight. We had started from the Moon. Earth and its planets quickly disappeared. We had seen the sun shrink till it was nothing but an orange in the sky, then a plum, and finally a point of light without dimensions, a simple star that only the professor's skill could distinguish from the millions of other stars in the galaxy.

We thus lived without sun, but were none the worse for this, the craft being equipped with equivalent sources of light. Nor were we bored. The professor's conversation was fascinating; I learned more during those two years than I had learned in all my previous existence. I also learned all that one needed to know in order to guide the spacecraft. It was fairly easy: one merely gave instructions to some electronic devices, which made all the calculations and directly initiated the maneuvers.

Our garden provided an agreeable distraction. It occupied an important place on board. Professor Antelle, who was interested, among other subjects, in botany and agriculture, had planned to take advantage of the voyage to check certain of his theories on the growth of plants in space. A cubic compartment with sides about thirty feet long served as a plot. Thanks to some trays, the whole of its volume was put to use. The earth was regenerated by means of chemical fertilizers and, scarcely more than two months after our departure, we had the pleasure of seeing it produce all sorts of vegetables, which provided us with an abundance of healthy food. Food for the eye, too, had not been forgotten: one section was reserved for flowers, which the professor tended lovingly. This eccentric had also brought some birds, butterflies, and even a monkey, a little chimpanzee whom we had christened Hector and who amused us with his tricks.

It is certain that the learned Antelle, without being a misanthrope, was not interested at all in human beings. He would often declare that he did not expect much from them any more, and this probably explains . . .

"Misanthrope?" Phyllis again broke in, dumbfounded. "Human beings?"

"If you keep interrupting me every other second," said Jinn, *"we shall never get to the end. Do as I do: try to understand."*

Phyllis promised to keep quiet till the end of the reading, and she kept her promise.

This probably explains why he had collected in the craft—which was big enough to accommodate several families—countless vegetable species and some animals, while limiting the number of the passengers to three: himself; his disciple Arthur Levain, a young physician with a great future; and myself, Ulysse Mérou, a little-known journalist who had met the professor as a result of an interview. He had suggested taking me with him after learning that I had no family and played chess reasonably well. This was an outstanding opportunity for a young journalist. Even if my story was not to be published for eight hundred years, perhaps for that very reason it would have unusual value. I had accepted with enthusiasm.

The voyage thus occurred without a setback. The only physical inconvenience was a sensation of heaviness during the year of acceleration and the one of reducing speed. We had to get used to feeling our bodies weigh one and a half times their weight on Earth, a somewhat tiring phenomenon to begin with, but to which we soon paid no attention. Between those two periods there was a complete absence of gravity, with all the oddities accruing from this phenomenon; but that lasted only a few hours and we were none the worse for it.

And one day, after this long crossing, we had the dazzling experience of seeing the star Betelgeuse appear in the sky in a new guise.

three

The feeling of awe produced by such a sight cannot be described: a star, which only yesterday was a brilliant speck among the multitude of anonymous specks in the firmament, showed up more and more clearly against the black background, assumed a dimension in space, appearing first of all as a sparkling nut, then swelled in size, at the same time becoming more definite in color, so that it resembled an orange, and finally fell into place in the cosmos with the same apparent diameter as our own familiar daytime star. A new sun was born for us, a reddish sun, like ours when it sets, the attraction and warmth of which we could already feel.

Our speed was then very much reduced. We drew still closer to Betelgeuse, until its apparent diameter

far exceeded that of all the heavenly bodies hitherto
seen, which made a tremendous impression on us.
Antelle gave some instructions to the robots and we
started gravitating around the supergiant. Then the
scientist took out his astronomical instruments and
began his observations.

It was not long before he discovered the existence
of four planets whose dimensions he rapidly determined, together with their distances from the central star. One of these, two away from Betelgeuse,
was moving on a trajectory parallel to ours. It was
about the same size as Earth; it possessed an atmosphere containing oxygen and nitrogen; it revolved
around Betelgeuse at a distance equivalent to thirty
times the space between the Sun and Earth, receiving a radiation comparable to that received by
our planet, thanks to the size of the supergiant combined with its relatively low temperature.

We decided to make it our first objective. After
fresh instructions were given to the robots, our craft
was quickly put into orbit around it. Then, with engines switched off, we observed this new world at
our leisure. The telescope revealed its oceans and
continents.

The craft was not equipped for a landing, but
this eventuality had been provided for. We had at
our disposal three much smaller rocket machines,
which we called launches. It was in one of these that
we embarked, taking with us some measuring instruments and Hector, the chimpanzee, who was

equipped as we were with a diving suit and had been trained in its use. As for our ship, we simply let it revolve around the planet. It was safer there than a liner lying at anchor in a harbor, and we knew it would not drift an inch from its orbit.

Landing on a planet of this kind was an easy operation with our launch. As soon as we had penetrated the thick layers of the atmosphere, Professor Antelle took some samples of the outside air and analyzed them. He found they had the same composition as the air on Earth at a similar altitude. I hardly had time to ponder on this miraculous coincidence, for the ground was approaching rapidly; we were no more than fifty miles or so above it. Since the robots carried out every maneuver, I had nothing to do but press my face to the porthole and watch this unknown world rising toward me, my brain reeling with the excitement of discovery.

The planet bore a strange resemblance to Earth. This impression became clearer every second. I could now discern the outline of the continents with my naked eye. The atmosphere was bright, slightly tinged with a pale green color verging from time to time on yellow, rather like our sky in Provence at sunset. The ocean was light blue, also with green tinges. The form of the coast line was very different from anything I had seen at home, though my feverish eye, conditioned by so many analogies, insisted wildly on discerning similarities even there. But there the resemblance ended. Nothing in the

planet's topography recalled either our Old or New
Worlds.

Nothing? Come now! On the contrary, the essential factor! The planet was inhabited. We flew over
a town: a fairly big town, from which roads radi-
ated, bordered with trees and with vehicles moving
along them. I had time to make out the general
architecture: broad streets and white houses with
long straight lines.

But we were to land a long way farther off. Our
flight swept us first over cultivated fields, then over
a thick russet-colored forest that called to mind our
equatorial jungle. We were now at a very low altitude. We caught sight of a fairly large clearing occupying the top of a plateau, the ground all around it
being rather broken. Our leader decided to attempt
a landing there and gave his last orders to the robots. A system of retrorockets came into action. We
hovered motionless for a moment or two above the
clearing, like a gull spotting a fish.

Then, two years after leaving our Earth, we came
down gently and landed without a jolt in the middle
of the plateau, on green grass reminiscent of our
meadows in Normandy.

four

We were silent and motionless for quite a time after making contact with the ground. Perhaps this behavior will seem surprising, but we felt the need to recover our wits and concentrate our energy. We were launched on an adventure a thousand times more extraordinary than that of the first terrestrial navigators and were preparing ourselves to confront the wonders of interstellar travel that have fired the imaginations of several generations of poets.

For the moment, talking of wonders, we had landed without a hitch on the grass of a planet that contained, as ours did, oceans, mountains, forests, cultivated fields, towns, and certainly inhabitants. Yet we must have been fairly far from the civilized regions, considering the stretch of jungle over which we had flown before touching down.

We eventually came out of our daydream. Having donned our diving suits, we carefully opened one porthole of the launch. There was no hiss of air. The pressures inside and outside were the same. The forest surrounded the clearing like the walls of a fortress. Not a sound, not a movement disturbed it. The temperature was high but bearable: about seventy-seven degrees Fahrenheit.

We climbed out of the launch, accompanied by Hector. Professor Antelle insisted first of all on analyzing the atmosphere by a more precise method. The result was encouraging: the air had the same composition as the Earth's, in spite of some differences in the proportion of the rare gases. It was undoubtedly breathable. Yet, to make doubly sure, we tried it out first on our chimpanzee. Rid of his suit, the monkey appeared perfectly happy and in no way inconvenienced. He seemed overjoyed to find himself free and on land. After a few skips and jumps, he scampered off to the forest, sprang into a tree, and continued his capering in the branches. He drew farther away and finally disappeared, ignoring our gestures and shouts.

Then, shedding our own space suits, we were able to talk easily. We were startled by the sound of our voices, and ventured only timidly to take a step or two without moving too far from our launch.

There was no doubt that we were on a twin planet

of our Earth. Life existed. The vegetable realm was, in fact, particularly lush: some of these trees must have been over a hundred and fifty feet tall. The animal kingdom soon appeared in the form of some big black birds, hovering in the sky like vultures, and other smaller ones, rather like parakeets, that chased one another chirping shrilly. From what we had seen before landing, we knew that a civilization existed, too. Rational beings—we dared not call them men yet—had molded the face of the planet. Yet the forest all around us appeared to be uninhabited. This was scarcely surprising; landing at random in some corner of the Asiatic jungle, we should have had the same impression of solitude.

Before taking a further step, we felt it was urgent to give the planet a name. We christened it Soror, because of its resemblance to our Earth.

Deciding to make an initial reconnaissance without delay, we entered the forest, following a sort of natural path. Arthur Levain and I were armed with carbines. As for the professor, he scorned material weapons. We felt light-footed and walked briskly: not that our weight was less than on Earth—there again the similarity was complete—but the contrast with the ship's force of gravity prompted us to scamper along like young goats.

We were marching in single file, calling out every now and then to Hector, but with no success, when young Levain, who was leading, stopped and motioned us to listen. A murmur, like running water, could be heard in the distance. We made our way in that direction and the sound became clearer.

It was a waterfall. On coming to it, all three of us were moved by the beauty of the site. A stream of water, clear as our mountain torrents, twisted above our heads, spread out into a sheet on a ledge of level ground, and fell at our feet from a height of several yards into a sort of lake, a natural swimming pool fringed with rocks mingled with sand, the surface of which reflected the light of Betelgeuse, which was then at its zenith.

The sight of this water was so tempting that the same urge seized both Levain and me. The heat was now intense. We took off our clothes and got ready to dive into the lake. But Professor Antelle cautioned us to behave with a little more prudence when coming up against the system of Betelgeuse for the first time. Perhaps this liquid was not water at all and might be extremely dangerous. He went up to the edge of it, bent down, examined it, then cautiously touched it with his finger. Finally he scooped a little up in the palm of his hand, smelled it, and wetted the end of his tongue with it.

"It can't be anything but water," he muttered.

He bent down again to plunge his hand into the lake, when we saw him suddenly stiffen. He gave an exclamation of surprise and pointed toward something he had just discerned in the sand. I experienced, I believe, the most violent emotion of my life. There, beneath the scorching rays of Betelgeuse that filled the sky above our heads like an enormous red balloon, visible to all of us and admirably outlined on a little patch of damp sand, was the print of a human foot.

five

"It's a woman's foot," Arthur Levain declared.

This peremptory remark, made in a strangled voice, did not surprise me at all. It confirmed my own opinion. The slimness, the elegance, the singular beauty of the footprint had disturbed me profoundly. There could be no doubt as to the humanness of the foot. Perhaps it belonged to an adolescent or to a small man, but with much more likelihood—and this I hoped with all my heart—to a woman.

"So Soror is inhabited by humans," Professor Antelle murmured.

There was a hint of disappointment in his voice, which made me at that moment less well disposed toward him. He shrugged his shoulders with a gesture that was habitual with him and joined us in inspecting the sand around the lake. We discovered other footprints, obviously left by the same creature. Levain, who had moved away from the water's edge, drew our attention to one on the dry sand. The print itself was still damp.

"She was here less than five minutes ago," the young man exclaimed.

"She was swimming, heard us coming, and fled."

It had become an implicit fact for us that the subject under discussion was a woman. We fell silent, scanning the forest, but without hearing so much as the noise of a branch breaking.

"We've got all the time in the world," said the professor, shrugging his shoulders again. "But if a human being swam here, we could no doubt do the same without any danger."

Without further ado the learned scientist shed his clothes and plunged his skinny body into the pool. After our long voyage the pleasure of this swim in cool, delicious water made us almost forget our recent discovery. Levain alone seemed harassed and lost in thought. I was about to make a taunting remark about his melancholy expression when I saw the woman just above us, perched on the rocky ledge from which the cascade fell.

I shall never forget the impression her appearance made on me. I held my breath at the marvelous beauty of this creature from Soror, who revealed herself to us dripping with spray, illuminated by the blood-red beams of Betelgeuse. It was a woman—a young girl, rather, unless it was a goddess. She boldly asserted her femininity in the light of this monstrous sun, completely naked and without any ornament other than her hair, which hung down to her shoulders. True, we had been deprived of any point of comparison for over two years, but none of us was inclined to fall a victim to mirages. It was plain to see that the woman, who stood motionless on the ledge like a statue on a pedestal, possessed the most perfect body that could be conceived on Earth. Levain and I were breathless, lost in admiration, and I think even Professor Antelle was moved.

Standing upright, leaning forward, her breasts thrust out toward us, her arms raised slightly backward in the attitude of a diver taking off, she was watching us, and her surprise clearly equaled our own. After gazing at her for a long time, I was so dazzled that I could not discern any particular feature: her body as a whole hypnotized me. It was only after several minutes that I saw she belonged to the white race, that her skin was golden rather than bronzed, that she was tall, but not excessively so, and slender. Then I noticed, as though in a dream, a face of singular purity. Finally I looked at her eyes.

Then I became more alert, my attention sharpened, and I stiffened, for in her expression there was an element that was new to me. In it I discerned the outlandish, mysterious quality all of us had been expecting in a world so distant from our own. But I was unable to analyze or even define the nature of this oddity. I only sensed an essential difference from individuals of our own species. It did not come from the color of her eyes: these were of a grayish hue not often found among us, but nevertheless not unknown. The anomaly lay in their emanation, a sort of void, an absence of expression, reminding me of a wretched mad girl I had once known. But no! it was not that, it could not be madness.

When she saw that she herself was an object of curiosity—or, to be more accurate, when my eyes met hers—she seemed to receive a shock and abruptly looked away with an automatic gesture as swift as that of a frightened animal. It was not out of shame at being thus scrutinized. I had a feeling that it would have been an exaggeration to suppose her capable of such an emotion. It was simply that her gaze would not, or could not, withstand mine. With her head turned to one side, she now watched us stealthily, out of the corner of her eye.

"As I told you, it's a woman," young Levain muttered.

He had spoken in a voice stifled with emotion, almost a whisper: but the young girl heard him and the sound of his voice produced a strange effect on her. She recoiled, but so swiftly that once again I compared her movement to the reflex of a frightened animal pausing before taking flight. She stopped, however, after taking two steps backward, the rocks then concealing most of her body. I could discern no more than the top of her head and an eye that was still trained on us.

We dared not move a muscle, tortured by the fear of seeing her rush away. Our attitude reassured her. After a moment she stepped out again onto the ledge. But young Levain was decidedly too excited to be able to hold his tongue.

"Never in my life . . ." he began.

He stopped, realizing his imprudence. She had recoiled in the same manner as before, as though the human voice terrified her.

Professor Antelle motioned us to keep quiet and started splashing about in the water without appearing to pay the slightest attention to her. We adopted the same tactics, which met with complete success. Not only did she step forward once more, but she soon showed a visible interest in our movements, an interest that was manifested in a rather unusual manner, rousing our curiosity even more. Have you ever watched a timid puppy on the beach while his master is swimming? He longs to join him in the water, but dares not. He takes three steps in one direction, three in another, draws away, scampers back, shakes his head, paws the ground. Such, exactly, was the behavior of this girl.

And all of a sudden we heard her: but the sounds she uttered only added to the impression of animality created by her attitude. She was then standing on the very edge of her perch, as though about to fling herself into the lake. She had broken off her

sort of dance for a moment. She opened her mouth.
I was standing a little to one side and was able to
study her without being noticed. I thought she was
going to speak, to give a shout. I was expecting
a cry. I was prepared for the most barbarous language, but not for the strange sounds that came out
of her throat; specifically out of her throat, for neither mouth nor tongue played any part in this sort
of shrill mewing or whining, which seemed yet
again to express the joyful frenzy of an animal. In
our zoos, sometimes, young chimpanzees play and
wrestle together giving just such little cries.

Since, despite our astonishment, we forced ourselves to go on swimming without paying attention
to her, she appeared to come to a decision. She lowered herself onto the rock, took a grip on it with her
hands, and started climbing down toward us. Her
agility was extraordinary. Her golden body, appearing to us through a cloud of spray and light, like
a fairy-tale vision, moved quickly down the rock
face along the thin transparent blade of the waterfall. In a few moments, clinging to some impercep-
tible projections, she was down at the level of the
lake, kneeling on a flat stone. She watched us a few
seconds longer, then took to the water and swam
toward us.

We realized she wanted to play and therefore
continued with our frolics, which had given her
such confidence, modifying our movements when-

ever she looked startled. Soon we were all involved in a game in which she had unconsciously laid down the rules: a strange game indeed, with a certain resemblance to the movements of seals in a pool, which consisted of alternately fleeing from us and approaching us, suddenly veering away when we were almost within reach, then drawing so close as to graze us but without every actually coming into contact. It was childish; but what would we not have done in order to tame the beautiful stranger! I noticed that Professor Antelle took part in this play with unconcealed pleasure.

This had been going on for some time, and we were getting out of breath, when I was struck by the paradoxical nature of the girl's expression: her solemnity. There she was, taking evident pleasure in the games she was inspiring, yet not a smile had appeared on her face. For some time this had given me a vague feeling of uneasiness, without my knowing exactly why. I was now relieved to discover the reason: she neither laughed nor smiled; from time to time she only uttered one of those little throaty crics that cvidently expressed her satisfaction.

I decided to make an experiment. As she approached me, cleaving the water with a peculiar swimming action resembling a dog's and with her hair streaming out behind her like the tail of a comet, I looked her straight in the eye and, before she could turn her head aside, gave her a smile filled with all the friendliness and affection I could muster.

The result was surprising. She stopped swimming, stood up in the water, which reached to her waist, and raised her hands in front of her in a gesture of defense. Then she quickly turned her back on me and raced for the shore. Out of the water she paused and half turned around, looking at me askance, as she had on the ledge, with the startled air of an animal that has just seen something alarming. Perhaps she might have regained her confidence, for the smile had frozen on my lips and I had started swimming again in an innocent manner, but a fresh incident renewed her emotion. We heard a noise in the forest and, tumbling from branch to branch, our friend Hector came into view, landed on his feet, and scampered over toward us, overjoyed at finding us again. I was amazed to see the bestial expression, compounded of fright and menace, that came over the young girl's face when she caught sight of the monkey. She drew back, hugging the rocks so closely as to melt into them, every muscle tensed, her back arched, her hands contracted like claws. All this because of a nice little chimpanzee who was about to greet us!

As he passed close by, without noticing her, she sprang out. Her body twanged like a bow. She seized him by the throat and closed her hands around his neck, holding the poor creature firmly between her thighs. Her attack was so swift that we did not even have time to intervene. The monkey hardly struggled. He stiffened after a few seconds and fell dead when she let go of him. This gorgeous creature—in a romantic flight of fancy I had christened her "Nova," able to compare her appearance only to that of a brilliant star—Nova had strangled a harmless pet animal with her own hands.

When, having recovered from our shock, we rushed toward her, it was far too late to save Hector. She turned to face us as though to defend herself, her arms again raised in front of her, her lips curled back, in a menacing attitude that brought us to a standstill. Then she uttered a last shrill cry, which could be interpreted as a shout of triumph or a bellow of rage, and fled into the forest. In a few seconds she had disappeared into the undergrowth that closed back around her golden body, leaving us standing aghast in the middle of the jungle, now completely silent once again.

six

"A female savage," I said, "belonging to some backward race like those found in New Guinea or in our African forests?"

I had spoken without the slightest conviction. Arthur Levain asked me, almost violently, if I had ever noted such grace and fineness of feature among primitive tribes. He was a hundred times right and I could think of nothing else to say. Professor Antelle, who appeared to be lost in thought, had nevertheless listened to our conversation.

"The most primitive people on our planet have a language," he finally said. "This girl cannot talk."

We searched for the stranger around the region of the stream, but unable to find the slightest trace of her, made our way back to our launch in the clearing.

The professor thought of taking off again to attempt a landing at some more civilized spot, but Levain suggested stopping where we were for at least twenty-four hours to try to establish another contact with this jungle's inhabitants. I supported him in this suggestion, which eventually prevailed. We dared not admit to one another that the hope of seeing the girl again held us to the area.

The afternoon went by without incident; but toward evening, after admiring the fantastic setting of Betelgeuse, which flooded the horizon beyond all human imagination, we had the impression of some change in our surroundings. The jungle gradually became alive with furtive rustlings and snappings, and we felt that invisible eyes were spying on us through the foliage. We spent an uneventful night, however, barricaded in our launch, keeping watch in turns. At dawn we experienced the same sensation, and I fancied I heard some shrill little cries like those Nova had uttered the day before. But none of the creatures with which our feverish imagination peopled the forest revealed itself.

So we decided to return to the waterfall. The entire way, we were obsessed by the unnerving impression of being followed and watched by creatures that dared not show themselves. Yet Nova, the day before, had been willing to approach us.

"Perhaps it's our clothes that frighten them," Arthur Levain said suddenly.

This seemed a most likely explanation. I distinctly remembered that when Nova had fled after strangling our monkey, she had found herself in front of our pile of clothes. She had then sprung aside quickly to avoid them, like a shy horse.

"We'll soon see."

And, diving into the lake after undressing, we started playing again as on the day before, ostensibly oblivious of all that surrounded us.

The same trick worked again. After a few minutes we noticed the girl on the rocky ledge, without having heard her approach. She was not alone. There was a man standing beside her, a man built like us, resembling men on Earth, a middle-aged man also completely naked, whose features were so similar to those of our goddess that I assumed he was her father. He was watching us, as she was, in an attitude of bewilderment and concern.

And there were many others. We noticed them little by little, while we forced ourselves to maintain our feigned indifference. They crept furtively out of the forest and gradually formed an unbroken circle around the lake. They were all sturdy, handsome specimens of humanity, men and women with golden skin, now looking restless, evidently prey to a great excitement and uttering an occasional sharp cry.

We were hemmed in and felt somewhat anxious, remembering the incident with the chimpanzee. But their attitude was not menacing; they simply appeared to be interested in our actions.

That was it. Presently Nova—Nova whom I already regarded as an old acquaintance—slipped into the water and the others followed one by one with varying degrees of hesitation. They all drew closer and we began to chase one another in the manner of seals as we had done the previous day; only now we were surrounded by a score or more of these strange creatures, splashing about and playing, all with solemn expressions contrasting oddly with these childish frolics.

After a quarter of an hour of this I was beginning to feel tired. Was it just to behave like school children that we had come all the way to the universe of Betelgeuse? I felt almost ashamed of myself and was vexed to see that the learned Antelle appeared to be taking great pleasure in this game. But what else could we do? It is hard to imagine the difficulty of establishing contact with creatures who are ignorant of the spoken word or of laughter. Yet I did my best. I went through a few motions that I hoped might convey some meaning. I clasped my hands in as friendly a manner as possible, bowing at the same time, rather like the Chinese. I waved kisses at them. None of these gestures evoked the least response. Not a glimmer of comprehension appeared in their eyes.

Whenever we had discussed, during the voyage,

our eventual encounter with living beings, we saw
in our mind's eye monstrous, misshapen creatures
of a physical aspect very different from ours, but we
always implicitly imagined the presence in them of
a *mind*. On the planet Soror reality appeared to be
quite the reverse: we had to do with inhabitants resembling us in every way from the physical point of
view but who appeared to be completely devoid of
the power of reason. This indeed was the meaning
of the expression I had found so disturbing in Nova
and that I now saw in all the others: a lack of con-
scious thought; the absence of intelligence.

They were interested only in playing. And even
then the game had to be pretty simple! With the
idea of introducing into it a semblance of coherence
that they could grasp, the three of us linked hands
and, with the water up to our waists, shuffled around
in a circle, raising and lowering our arms together as
small children might have done. This seemed not to
move them in the slightest. Most of them drew away
from us; others gazed at us with such an obvious
absence of comprehension that we were ourselves
dumfounded.

It was the intensity of our dismay that gave rise to
the tragedy. We were so amazed to find ourselves,
three grown men, one of whom was a world celebrity,
holding hands while executing a childish dance under
the mocking eye of Betelgeuse, that we were unable to
keep straight faces. We had undergone such restraint

for the last quarter of an hour that we needed some relief. We were overcome by bursts of wild and uncontrollable laughter.

This explosion of hilarity at last awakened a response in the onlookers, but certainly not the one we had been hoping for. A sort of tempest ruffled the lake. They started rushing off in all directions in a state of fright that in other circumstances would have struck us as laughable. After a few moments we found ourselves alone in the water. They ended up by collecting together on the bank at the edge of the pool, in a trembling mob, uttering their furious little cries and stretching their arms out toward us in rage. Their gestures were so menacing that we took fright. Levain and I made for our weapons, but the wise Antelle whispered to us not to use them and even not to brandish them so long as they did not approach us.

We hastily dressed without taking our eyes off them. But scarcely had we put on our trousers and shirts than their agitation grew into a frenzy. It appeared that the sight of men wearing clothes was unbearable to them. Some of them took to their heels; others advanced toward us, their arms outstretched, their hands clawing the air. I picked up my carbine. Paradoxically for such obtuse people, they seemed to grasp the meaning of this gesture, turned tail, and disappeared into the trees.

We made haste to regain the launch. On our way

back I had the impression that they were still there, albeit invisible, and were following our withdrawal in silence.

seven

The attack was launched as we came within sight of the clearing, with an abruptness that precluded all defense. Leaping out of the thickets like stags, the men of Soror were upon us before we could lift our weapons to our shoulders.

The curious thing about this aggression was that it was not exactly directed against our persons. I sensed this at once, and my intuition was soon confirmed. At no moment did I feel myself in danger of death, as Hector had been. They were not after our lives, but after our clothes and all the accessories we were carrying. In a moment we were overwhelmed. A mass of probing hands stripped us of our weapons and ammunition pouches and threw these aside, while others struggled to peel off our clothes and tear them to shreds. Once I had understood what had provoked their fury, I passively gave in, and though I received a few scratches I was not seriously injured. Antelle and Levain did the same, and presently we found ourselves stark naked in the midst of a group of men and women who, visibly reassured to see us in this state, started dancing around us, encircling us too tightly for us to be able to escape.

There were now at least a hundred of them on the edge of the clearing. Those who were farther away then fell upon our launch with a fury comparable to that which had induced them to pull our clothes to pieces. In spite of the despair I felt at seeing them pillage our precious vehicle, I pondered on their behavior and fancied I could discern an essential principle in it: these beings were roused to fury by *objects*. Things that were *manufactured* provoked their anger as well as their fear. When they seized an instrument, they held it in their hands only long enough to break it, tear it apart, or twist it. Then they promptly hurled it as far away as possible, as though it were a live coal, only to pick it up again and complete its destruction. They made me think of a cat fighting with a big rat that was half dead but still dangerous, or of a mongoose that had caught a snake. I had already noted the curious fact that they had attacked us without a single weapon, without even using sticks.

Powerless, we witnessed the sacking of our launch. The door had soon yielded to their blows. They rushed inside and destroyed everything that could be destroyed, in particular the precious navigating instruments, and scattered the bits and pieces. This pillage lasted quite a time. Then, since the metal envelope alone remained intact, they came back to our group. We were jostled, pulled this way and that, and finally dragged off into the depths of the jungle.

Our situation was becoming more and more alarming. Disarmed, stripped, obliged to march barefoot at too fast a pace, we could neither exchange our impressions nor even complain. The slightest attempt at conversation provoked such menacing reactions that we had to resign ourselves to painful silence. And yet these creatures were men like us. Clad and shod, they would scarcely have drawn attention in our world. Their women were all beautiful, though none could rival Nova's splendor.

The latter followed close behind us. On several occasions, when I was jostled by my guards, I turned around toward her, imploring a sign of compassion, which I fancied I discerned once on her face. But this, I think, was only wishful thinking. As soon as my gaze met hers, she tried to avoid it, without her eyes expressing any sentiment other than bewilderment.

This calvary lasted several hours. I was overwhelmed with fatigue, my feet bleeding, my body covered with scratches caused by the reeds through which these men of Soror made their way with impunity, like snakes. My companions were in no better shape than I was, and Antelle was stumbling at every step by the time we finally reached what appeared to be the end of the march. The forest was less thick at this spot and the undergrowth had given place to short grass. Here our guards released us and, without bothering about us, started playing once more, chasing one another through the trees, which seemed to be their main occupation. We sank to the ground, numb with fatigue, taking advantage of this respite to hold a consultation.

It needed all the philosophy of our leader to prevent us from being engulfed in dark despair. Night was falling. We could no doubt attempt an escape by taking advantage of the general inattention; but then what? Even if we managed to retrace our steps, there was no chance of our being able to use the launch. It seemed wiser to remain where we were and to try to win over these disconcerting beings. Moreover, we were famished.

We rose to our feet and took a few timid steps. They went on with their senseless games without paying any attention. Nova alone seemed not to have forgotten us. She started following us at a distance, always turning her head away when we looked at her. After wandering at random, we discovered we were in a sort of encampment where the shelters were not even huts, but nestlike constructions like those built by the big apes in our African forests: a few interwoven branches, without any binding, placed on the ground or wedged into the forks of low trees. Some of these nests were occupied. Men and women—I cannot see how else I can describe them—lay stretched out inside them, often in couples, fast asleep and snuggling up together as dogs do in the cold. Other, larger shelters served entire families, and we noticed several children who looked extremely handsome and healthy.

This provided no solution to our feeding problem. At last we saw at the foot of a tree a family getting ready to eat, but their meal was hardly designed to tempt us. They were pulling to pieces, without the aid of any utensil, a fairly large animal resembling a deer. With their nails and their teeth they tore off bits of the raw meat, which they devoured after merely removing a few shreds of skin. There was no sign of a fireplace in the neighborhood. This feast turned our stomachs, and in any case, after drawing a little closer, we realized we were by no means welcome to share it. Quite the contrary! Angry growls made us draw back quickly.

It was Nova who came to our rescue. Did she do so because she had finally understood that we were hungry? Could she really *understand* anything? Or was it because she was famished herself? In any case, she went up to a big tree, encircled the trunk with her thighs, climbed up into the branches, and disappeared in the foliage. A few moments later we saw a shower of fruit resembling bananas fall to the ground. Then she climbed down again, picked up one or two of these and began eating them without taking her eyes off us. After a moment's hesitation we grew bold enough to imitate her. The fruit was quite good and we were able to eat our fill while she watched us without protesting. After drinking some water from a stream, we decided to spend the night there.

Each of us chose a corner in the grass in which to build a nest similar to the others in the colony. Nova showed some interest in our work, even to the point of approaching me and helping me to break a recalcitrant branch.

I was moved by this gesture; young Levain found it so vexing that he lay down at once, buried himself in the grass, and turned his back on us. As for Professor Antelle, he had already fallen asleep, dead tired.

I took some time to finish my bed, still closely watched by Nova, who had drawn some distance away. When I lay down, she stood motionless for a moment or two, as though unable to make up her mind; then she took a few hesitant steps toward me. I did not move a muscle for fear of frightening her away. She lay down beside me. I still did not move. She eventually snuggled up against me, and there was nothing to distinguish us from the other couples occupying the nests of this strange tribe. But although this girl was marvelously beautiful, I still did not regard her as a woman. Her manner was that of a pet animal seeking the warmth of its master. I appreciated the warmth of her body, without its ever crossing my mind to desire her. I ended up by falling asleep in this outlandish position, half dead from fatigue, pressed against this strangely beautiful and unbelievably mindless creature, after bestowing no more than a glance on the satellite of Soror, which, smaller than our Moon, cast a yellowish light over the jungle.

eight

The sky was turning pale through the trees when I awoke. Nova was still asleep. I watched her in silence and sighed as I remembered her cruelty to our poor monkey. She had probably also been the cause of our misadventure by pointing us out to her companions. But how could one hold this against her when faced with the perfection of her body?

Suddenly she stirred and raised her head. A gleam of fear came into her eyes and I felt her muscles contract. Since I did not move, however, her face gradually relaxed. She remembered; she managed for the first time to withstand my gaze for a moment. I regarded this as a personal victory and went so far as to smile at her again, forgetting her previous reaction to this earthly manifestation.

This time it was less intense. She shivered, stiffened again as though about to take flight, but stayed where she was. Encouraged, I smiled more broadly. She trembled again but eventually calmed down, her face soon expressing nothing but profound astonishment. Had I succeeded in taming her? I became bold enough to put my hand on her shoulder. A shiver ran down her spine, but she still did not move. I was intoxicated by this success, and was even more so when I thought she was trying to imitate me.

It was true. She was *trying* to smile. I could sense her painful efforts to contract the muscles of her delicate face. She made several attempts, managing only to produce a sort of painful grimace. There was something tremendously moving about this excessive labor on the part of a human being to achieve an everyday expression, and with such a pitiful result. I suddenly felt extremely touched, filled with compassion as though for a crippled child. I increased the pressure of my hand on her shoulder. I brought my face closer to hers. She replied to this gesture by rubbing her nose against mine, then by passing her tongue over my cheek.

I was bewildered and hesitant. To be on the safe side, I imitated her in my clumsy fashion. After all, I was a foreign visitor and it was up to me to adopt the customs of the great Betelgeuse system. She appeared satisfied. We had gone thus far in our attempts at communication, myself none too sure how to continue, frightened of committing some blunder with my Earthly manners, when a terrifying hullabaloo made us start up in alarm.

I found myself with my two companions, whom I had selfishly forgotten, standing bolt upright in the gathering dawn. Nova had sprung to her feet even more quickly and showed signs of the deepest terror. I understood immediately that this din was a nasty surprise not only for us but for all the inhabitants of the forest, for all of them, abandoning their lairs, had started running hither and thither in panic. This was not a game, as on the previous day; their cries expressed sheer terror.

This din, suddenly breaking the silence of the forest, was enough to make one's blood run cold, but I felt besides that the men of the jungle knew what was in the offing and that their fear was caused by the approach of a specific danger. It was a strange cacophony, a mixture of rattling sounds like a roll of drums, other more discordant noises resembling a clashing of pots and pans, and also shouts. It was the shouts that made the most impression on us, for although they were in no language familiar to us, they were incontestably *human*.

The early morning light revealed a strange scene in the forest: men, women, and children running in all directions, passing and bumping into one another, some of them even climbing into the trees as though to seek refuge there. Soon, however, some of the older ones stopped to prick up their ears and listen. The noise was approaching rather slowly. It came from the region where the forest was thickest and seemed to emanate from a fairly long unbroken line. I compared it to the noise made by beaters in one of our big shoots.

The elders of the tribe appeared to make a decision. They uttered a series of yelps, which were no doubt signals or orders, then rushed off in the opposite direction from the noise. The rest of them followed, and we saw them galloping all round us like a driven herd of deer. Nova, too, was about to take to her heels, but she paused suddenly and turned around toward us—above all toward me, I felt. She uttered a plaintive whimper, which I assumed to be an invitation to follow her, then took one leap and disappeared.

The din grew louder and I fancied I heard the undergrowth snapping as though beneath some heavy footsteps. I admit that I lost my composure. Caution prompted me, however, to stay where I was and to face the newcomers who, it became clearer every second, were uttering these human cries. But after my ordeal of the day before, this horrible racket unnerved me. I was infected by the terror of Nova and the others. I did not pause to think; I did not even wait to consult my companions; I plunged into the undergrowth and took to my heels in the young girl's footsteps.

I ran as fast as I could for several hundred yards without being able to catch up with her, and then noticed that Levain alone had followed me, Professor Antelle's age precluding such rapid flight. Levain was panting beside me. We looked at each other, ashamed of our behavior, and I was about to suggest going back or at least waiting for our leader, when some other noises made us jump in alarm.

As to these, I could not be mistaken. They were gunshots echoing through the jungle: one, two, three, then several more, at irregular intervals, sometimes one at a time, at other times two consecutive shots, strangely reminiscent of a double-barreled gun. They were firing in front of us, on the path taken by the fugitives. While we paused, the line from which the first din had come, the line of beaters, drew closer, very close to us, sowing panic in us once again. I do not know why the shooting seemed to me less frightening, more familiar than this hellish din. Instinctively I resumed my headlong flight, taking care nevertheless to keep under cover of the undergrowth and to make as little noise as possible. My companion followed after me.

We thus reached the region in which the shots had been heard. I slowed down and crept forward, almost on all fours. Still followed by Levain, I clambered up a sort of hillock and came to a halt on the summit, panting for breath. There was nothing in front of me but a few trees and a curtain of scrub. I advanced cautiously, my head on a level with the ground. There I lay for a moment or two as though floored by a blow, overpowered by a spectacle completely beyond my poor human comprehension.

nine

There were several incongruous features in the scene that unfolded before my eyes, some of them horrifying, but my attention was at first drawn exclusively to a figure standing motionless thirty paces away and peering in my direction.

I almost shouted aloud in amazement. Yes, in spite of my terror, in spite of the tragedy of my own position—I was caught between the beaters and the guns—stupefaction overrode all other emotion when I saw this creature on the lookout, lying in wait for the game. For it was an ape, a large-sized gorilla. It was in vain that I told myself I was losing my reason: I could entertain not the slightest doubt as to his species. But an encounter with a gorilla on the planet Soror was not the essential outlandishness of the situation. This for me lay in the fact that the ape was correctly dressed, like a man of our world, and above all that he wore his clothes in such an easy manner. This *natural* aspect was what struck me first of all. No sooner had I seen the animal than I realized that he was not in any way *disguised*. The state in which I saw him was normal, as normal to him as nakedness was to Nova and her companions.

He was dressed as you and I are, I mean as you and I would be if we were taking part in one of those drives organized for ambassadors or other distinguished persons at official shooting parties. His dark-brown jacket seemed to be made by the best Paris tailor and revealed underneath a checked shirt of the kind our sportsmen wear. His breeches, flaring out slightly above his calves, terminated in a pair of leggings. There the resemblance ended: instead of boots he wore big black gloves.

It was a gorilla, I tell you! From his shirt collar emerged a hideous head, its top shaped like a sugar loaf and covered with black hair, with a flattened nose and jutting jaws. There he stood, leaning slightly forward, in the posture of a hunter on the lookout, grasping a rifle in his long hands. He was facing me, on the other side of a large gap cut out of the jungle at right angles to the direction of the drive.

All of a sudden he stiffened. He had noticed, as I had, a faint sound in the bushes a little to my right.

He turned around and at the same time raised his weapon, ready to put it to his shoulder. From my position I could see the furrow left in the undergrowth by one of the fugitives who was running blindly straight ahead. I almost shouted out to warn him, so obvious was the ape's intention. But I had neither the time nor the strength; the man was already racing like a mountain goat across the open ground. The shot rang out while he was still halfway across the field of fire. He gave a leap in the air, collapsed in a heap on the ground, and after a few convulsions lay motionless.

But it was only a little later that I noticed the victim's death agony, my attention being still focused on the gorilla. I had followed the changes in his expression from the moment he was alerted by the noise, and had noted a number of surprising facts: first, the cruelty of the hunter stalking his prey and the feverish pleasure he derived from this pastime; but above all, the *human* character of his expression—in this animal's eyes there was a spark of understanding that I had sought in vain among the men of Soror.

The realization of my own position soon roused me from my stupor. The shot made me turn my gaze again toward the victim, and I was the horrified witness of his final twitches. I then noticed with terror that the cleared space in the forest was littered with human bodies. It was no longer possible to delude myself as to the meaning of this scene. I caught sight of another gorilla like the first one, a hundred paces off. I was witnessing a drive—alas, I was taking part in it!—a fantastic drive in which the guns, posted at regular intervals, were apes and the game consisted of men, men like me, men and women whose naked, punctured bodies, twisted in ridiculous postures, lay bleeding on the ground.

I turned aside from this unbearable horror. I preferred the sight of the merely grotesque, and I gazed back at the gorilla barring my path. He had taken a step to one side, revealing another ape standing behind him, like a servant beside his master. It was a chimpanzee, a rather small chimpanzee, a young chimpanzee, it seemed to me, but a chimpanzee, I swear, dressed with less elegance than the gorilla, in a pair of trousers and a shirt, and easily playing his part in the meticulous organization that I was beginning to discern. The hunter had just handed him his gun. The chimpanzee exchanged it for another he was holding in his hand. Then, with precise gestures, using the cartridges in the belt he was wearing around his waist and that sparkled in the rays of Betelgeuse, the little chimpanzee reloaded the weapon. Then each resumed his position.

All these impressions had taken only a few seconds. I should have liked to think about these discoveries, to analyze them; I had no time to do so. Lying beside me, Arthur Levain, numb with terror, was incapable of giving me the slightest help. The danger was increasing at every second. The beaters

were approaching from behind. The din they made
was now deafening. We were at bay like wild beasts,
like those wretched creatures whom I still see flitting
all around us. The size of the colony must have been
bigger than I had suspected, for many men were still
rushing along the track, to meet there a ghastly
death.

Not all, however. Forcing myself to recover a
little composure, from the top of my hillock I
studied the behavior of the fugitives. Some of them,
completely panic-stricken, rushed along snapping
the undergrowth in their flight, thus alerting the
apes, who easily shot them down. But others gave
evidence of more cunning, like old boars who have
been hunted several times and have learned a
number of tricks. These crept forward on all fours,
paused for a moment on the edge of the clearing,
studied the nearest hunter through the leaves, and
waited for the moment when his attention was
drawn in another direction. Then, in one bound
and at full speed, they crossed the deadly alley.
Several of them thus succeeded in reaching the opposite side unhurt, and disappeared into the forest.

Therein perhaps lay a chance of safety. I motioned
to Levain to follow me and slipped soundlessly forward as far as the last thicket in front of the path.
There I was overwhelmed by a ridiculous scruple.
Should I, a man, really resort to such tricks merely
to get the better of an ape? Surely the only behavior
worthy of my condition was to rise to my feet,

advance on the animal, and give it a good beating? The ever-increasing hullabaloo behind me reduced this mad inclination to nought.

The hunt was ending in an infernal din. The beaters were at our heels. I saw one of them emerge from the foliage. It was an enormous gorilla, laying about him at random with a club and screeching fit to burst his lungs. He made an even more terrifying impression on me than the hunter with the gun. Levain started chattering with fear and trembling from head to foot, while I kept my eye on the new-comer in front of me and waited for an opportune moment.

My wretched companion unconsciously saved my life by his imprudence. He had gone completely out of his mind. He got up without taking any pre-caution, started running off at random, and came out into the alley in full view of the hunter's field of fire. He went no farther. The shot seemed to snap him in two and he collapsed, adding his body to all those that already lay there. I wasted no time in mourning him—what could I do for him?—but waited feverishly for the moment when the gorilla would hand his gun to his servant. As soon as he did so, I sprang out and raced across the alley. I saw the hunter, as though in a dream, hasten to seize his weapon, but I was already under cover by the time he could lift it to his shoulder. I heard an exclama-tion that sounded like an oath, but had no time for thought about this latest oddity.

I had got the best of him. I felt a strange joy, which was balm to my humiliation. I went on running at full speed, leaving the carnage behind me, until I could not longer hear the noise of the beaters. I was saved.

Saved! I was underestimating the maliciousness of the apes on the planet Soror. Hardly had I gone a hundred yards when I stumbled headfirst into an obstacle concealed in the foliage. It was a wide-meshed net stretched above the ground and equipped with large pockets, in one of which I was now entangled. I was not the only captive. The net ran across a large section of the forest, and a crowd of fugitives who had escaped being shot had let themselves be caught as I had. To my right and left frenzied jerks accompanied by furious whines bore witness to their efforts to break free.

A wild rage overcame me when I felt myself thus imprisoned, a rage stronger than terror, leaving me utterly incapable of thought. I did exactly what my reason advised me not to do—I struggled in an utterly insanc manner, with the result that the net became even more tightly wound around me. I was eventually so closely bound that I could not move at all and was at the mercy of the apes I heard approaching.

ten

I was seized by a deadly terror when I saw their troop advancing. After witnessing their cruelty, I thought they were going to engage in wholesale massacre.

The hunters, all of them gorillas, led the advance. I noticed that they had abandoned their weapons, which gave me a little hope. Behind them came the loaders and beaters, among whom there was a more or less equal number of gorillas and chimpanzees. The hunters seemed to be the masters and their manner was that of aristocrats. They did not appear to be ill-disposed, and chatted among themselves as cheerfully as one could wish. . . .

In fact, I am now so accustomed to the paradoxes of this planet that I wrote the preceding sentence without thinking of the absurdity it represents. And yet it's the truth! The gorillas had the manner of aristocrats. They chatted together happily in an articulate language, and each moment their faces expressed human sentiments, not a trace of which I had found in Nova. Alas! What had become of Nova? I shuddered as I recalled the bloodstained alley. I now understood her emotion at the sight of our chimpanzee. There existed a fierce hatred between the two races. To realize this one only had to see the attitude of the captive men at the apes' approach. They struggled frenziedly, thrashing out with hands and feet, ground their teeth, foamed at the mouth, and gnawed furiously at the strings of the net.

Without paying attention to this hubbub, the hunter gorillas—I caught myself calling them the nobility—gave some orders to their servants. Some big carts, rather low-lying and completely caged in, were lined up on a track on the other side of the net. Into these we were bundled, ten or so to a vehicle: a fairly lengthy operation, for the prisoners struggled desperately. Two servant gorillas, their hands encased in leather gloves to protect them from bites, took hold of the prisoners one by one, freed them from the trap, and flung them into the cages, the doors of which were then shut fast, while the nobles directed the operation leaning negligently on their walking sticks.

When it came to my turn, I tried to draw attention to myself by talking. But no sooner had I opened my mouth than one of the apes, no doubt mistaking my action for a menace, brutally stuffed his enormous glove into my face. I was forcibly silenced and thrown like a bundle into a cage together with a dozen men and women who were still too agitated to pay any attention to me.

When we were all loaded inside, one of the servants checked the lock on each cage and went to report to his master. The latter gave a signal, and a roar of engines echoed through the forest. The carts started to move forward, each one towed by a sort of tractor driven by an ape. I could distinctly see the driver of the vehicle behind mine. He was a chimpanzee. From time to time he made sarcastic remarks at us, and when the engines slowed down I could hear him humming a rather melancholy little tune not altogether lacking in harmony.

This first stage was so short that I scarcely had time to recover my senses. After driving for a quarter of an hour along a rough track, the convoy came to a halt on a stretch of open ground in front of a house built of stone. It was the edge of the forest; beyond it I could see a plain covered with crops that looked like cereals.

The house, with its red tiled roof, green shutters, and an inscription on a panel at the entrance, looked like an inn. I realized at once it was a meeting place for the hunt. The she-apes had come here to wait for their lords and masters, who presently arrived in private cars along the same track we had taken. The lady gorillas sat around in armchairs chatting together in the shade of some big trees that looked like palms. One of them was sipping a drink through a straw.

As soon as the vehicles were parked, the females drew nearer, curious to see the results of the hunt and especially the game that had been shot, which some gorillas, protected by aprons, were extracting from two big vans to display in the shade of the trees.

It was a classical hunting scene. Here again the apes worked methodically. They placed the bleeding bodies on their backs, side by side, in a long row as though along a chalk line. Then, while the she-apes uttered little cries of admiration, they applied themselves to making the game attractive. They stretched the arms down along the sides of the bodies and opened the hands with the palms facing upward. They straightened the legs, arranging the joints so as to give each body a less corpselike appearance, corrected a clumsily twisted limb, and reduced the contraction of a neck. Then they carefully smoothed down the hair, particularly the women's, as some hunters smooth down the coat or feathers of an animal they have just shot.

I am afraid I am unable to convey the grotesque and diabolical quality this scene had for me. Have I adequately stressed the absolutely and totally *simian* appearance of these monkeys, apart from the expression in their eyes? Have I described how these she-gorillas, also dressed in sports clothes but with great elegance, jostled one another to view the best specimens and point them out while congratulating their lords and masters? Have I said that one of them, taking a little pair of scissors out of her bag, leaned over a body, cut off a lock of brown hair, curled it around her finger, and then, with the others soon following her example, pinned it onto her hat?

The exhibition of the game was soon completed: three rows of bodies carefully laid out, men and women alternately, the latter displaying a line of golden breasts to the monstrous sphere blazing in the sky. Looking away in horror, I noticed a new figure, carrying an oblong box fastened to a tripod. It was a chimpanzee. I quickly recognized in him the photographer making a pictorial record and these trophies for simian posterity. The session lasted more than a quarter of an hour, the gorillas having themselves photographed first individually, in good poses, some of them placing one foot on one of their victims with a triumphant air; then as a compact group, each of them putting an arm around his neighbor's shoulder. The she-gorillas in turn were then photographed and assumed graceful postures in front of the slaughter, with their decorated hats well to the fore.

This scene was imbued with a horror incomprehensible to the normal mind. My blood boiled, but I succeeded for some time in restraining myself. However, when I noticed the body on which one of these females had sat down to take a more sensational picture, when I recognized on the face of the corpse stretched out among the others the boyish, almost childish features of my luckless companion, Arthur Levain, it was no longer possible to contain myself. My emotion exploded in an outlandish manner, in keeping with the grotesque aspect of this macabre scene. I gave way to a fit of wild hilarity, bursting out in hysterical laughter.

I had not thought of my companions in the cage. I was utterly incapable of thinking! The tumult unleashed by my laughter reminded me of their proximity, which was no doubt as dangerous for me as that of the apes. Menacing hands were stretched in my direction. I realized the peril and stifled my laughter by burying my head in my arms. I am not sure, however, that I should have avoided being strangled and torn to bits if some of the apes, alarmed by the din, had not re-established order with a few thrusts of their pikes. Moreover, another incident soon diverted the general attention. The gorillas made their way in small groups toward the house, chatting merrily together, while the photographer gathered up his equipment after taking a few shots of our cages.

We men, however, had not been forgotten. I had no idea of the fate the monkeys had in store for us, but it was clearly their policy to look after us. Before disappearing into the inn, one of the nobles gave some instructions to a gorilla who appeared to be a team leader. The latter came over to us, assembled his subordinates, and presently the servants brought us something to eat in basins and some buckets of water to drink. The food consisted of a sort of porridge. I was not hungry but was determined to eat in order to keep up my strength. I approached one of the receptacles around which several prisoners were squatting. I did as they did and stretched out a timid hand. They gave me a surly look but, the food being ample, did not try to stop me. It was a thick mash with a cereal base that did not taste bad. I swallowed several handfuls without displeasure.

Our menu was, moreover, enriched by the good will of our guards. Now that the hunt was over, these beaters, who had so frightened me, proved to be less unpleasant so long as we behaved ourselves. They walked up and down in front of the cages and threw us some fruit from time to time, deriving great amusement from the stampede these offerings never failed to provoke. I even witnessed a scene that gave me food for thought. A little girl had caught a piece of fruit in the air, when her neighbor rushed at her to snatch it away. One of the gorillas then brandished his pike, poked it through the bars, and pushed the man back as hard as he could; then he put another bit of fruit in the same child's hand. I thus realized that these creatures were capable of pity.

When the meal was over, the team leader and his assistants set about rearranging the convoy by transferring some of the captives from one cage to

another. They seemed to be making some sort of selection, but on what basis I could not tell. Finding
myself placed in a group of extremely handsome
men and women, I tried to persuade myself that this
was because we were the most remarkable subjects,
deriving a bitter consolation from the thought that
the apes, at first glance had judged me worthy of
being included in an élite.

I was surprised and overjoyed to see Nova among
my new companions. She had escaped the massacre
and I gave thanks to the heaven of Betelgeuse. It was
with her, above all, in mind that I had scrutinized the
victims at great length, fearful of seeing at any moment her lovely body among the pile of corpses. I
felt as though I had recovered a being that was dear
to me and, losing my head once more, I rushed over
to her, opening my arms wide. It was utter madness;
my gesture terrified her. Had she forgotten, then,
our intimacy of the night before? Was such a marvelous physique not animated by any sort of mind? I
felt downcast to see her shrink away at my approach, her hands extended like claws as though to
throttle me, which she probably would have done
had I persisted.

Yet when I checked myself she calmed down
fairly quickly. She lay down in a corner of the cage
and I followed her example with a sigh. All the
other captives had done likewise. They now looked
listless, prostrate, and resigned to their fate.

Outside, the apes were getting ready for the convoy

to move off. A tarpaulin was stretched over our cage and fastened halfway down the sides, letting in some light. Orders were issued; the engines started. I found myself traveling at high speed toward an unknown destination, terrified by the thought of the fresh horrors that awaited me on the planet Soror.

eleven

I was utterly exhausted. The events of the last two days had broken me physically and plunged my mind into such confusion that I had been incapable until now of bewailing the loss of my comrades or even of picturing concretely all that was involved for me in the pillaging of our launch. It was with relief that I welcomed the half-light, then isolation in the almost total darkness that followed, for the dusk was very swift and we drove all through the night. I racked my brains to discover some sense in the events I had witnessed. I needed this intellectual exercise to escape from the despair that haunted me, to prove to myself that I was a man, I mean a man from Earth, a reasoning creature who made it a habit to discover a logical explanation for the apparently miraculous whims of nature, and not a beast hunted down by highly developed apes.

I reviewed all that I had observed, often without being aware of it. A general overall impression prevailed: these apes, male and female, gorillas and chimpanzees, were not in any way *ridiculous*. I have already mentioned that they had never struck me as being animals in disguise, like the tame monkeys exhibited in our circuses. On Earth a hat on the head of a she-monkey was a hilarious sight to some people, to me a painful one. Not so here. Both head and hat were in keeping, and there was nothing at all unnatural about any of their gestures. The she-ape sipping a drink through a straw looked like a lady. I also remember having seen one of the hunters take a pipe out of his pocket, fill it methodically, and light it. Well, nothing about this act had shocked my sensibilities, so natural were his movements. I had had to think about it before recognizing it as a paradox. I pondered over this at great length and, for the first time since my capture, I deplored the disappearance of Professor Antelle. In his wisdom and knowledge he would doubtless have been able to find an explanation for these paradoxes. What had become of him? I was certain he was not among the victims that had been shot. Was he among the captives? It was not impossible; I had not seen them all. I dared not hope that he had succeeded in preserving his liberty.

With my feeble resources I tried to piece together

an hypothesis, but it was not very satisfactory. Could the inhabitants of this planet, the civilized beings whose towns we had seen, could they have succeeded in training apes so as to instill more or less rational behavior in them—this, after patient selection and efforts lasting several generations? After all, on Earth there are chimpanzees who manage to perform astonishing tricks. The very fact that they had a language was perhaps not so outlandish as I had thought. I now remembered a discussion I had had on this subject with a specialist. He had told me there were learned scientists who spent a large part of their time trying to teach primates to talk. They claimed that there was nothing in the conformation of these animals to prevent it. Until then all their efforts had been in vain, but they were persevering, maintaining that the only obstacle was the fact that monkeys were *unwilling* to talk. Perhaps one day they had proved willing on the planet Soror? This enabled these hypothetical inhabitants to use them for certain rough work, like the hunt during which I had been captured.

I clung desperately to this explanation, recoiling in horror at the thought of another, simpler one, so essential for my safety did it seem that there should exist on this planet properly rational creatures, that is, men, men like myself, to whom I could reveal myself.

Men! Of what race, then, were the beings whom

the apes had killed and captured? Some sort of backward tribe? If that were the case, how cruel the masters of this planet were to tolerate and perhaps decree such massacres!

I was distracted from these thoughts by a figure creeping toward me. It was Nova. Around me, all the prisoners were lying in groups on the floor boards. After a moment's hesitation she snuggled up against me, as on the previous night. Once again I vainly tried to discern in her eyes the gleam by which this gesture of hers might have been construed as an act of friendliness. She turned her head away and presently closed her eyes. In spite of this I felt reassured by her mere presence and eventually fell asleep beside her, trying not to think of the morrow.

twelve

I succeeded in sleeping till daybreak through a defense mechanism against the intrusion of thoughts that were too unbearable. My sleep was interrupted, however, by feverish nightmares, in which Nova's body appeared in the guise of a monstrous serpent wound around my own body. I opened my eyes to the light. She was already awake. She had drawn a little away from me and was watching me with her eternally bewildered gaze.

Our vehicle slowed down and I saw we were entering a town. The captives had risen and were squatting beside the bars, glancing out beneath the tarpaulin at a spectacle that seemed to revive their emotions of the previous day. I followed their example; I pressed my face against the bars and for the first time viewed a civilized city on the planet Soror.

We were driving down a fairly broad street flanked with pavements. I anxiously examined the passersby: they were apes. I saw a tradesman, a sort of grocer, who had just raised the shutters of his shop, turn around curiously to watch us go by; he was an ape. I tried to see the passengers and drivers of the motor cars flashing past us: they were dressed in the same way as people at home and they were apes.

My hope of discovering a civilized human race became chimerical, and I spent the last part of the drive in gloomy despair. Our vehicle slowed down even more. I then noticed that the convoy had been split up during the night, for it consisted of only two vehicles, the others evidently having taken another direction. After passing through an entrance gate we came to a halt in a courtyard. Some apes immediately surrounded us and tried to calm down the captives' mounting agitation with a few blows of their pikes.

The courtyard was enclosed by buildings several stories high with identical rows of windows. The general effect was that of a hospital, and this impression was confirmed by the arrival of some new figures who came forward to meet our guards. They were all dressed in white smocks and little caps: they were apes.

They were apes, every one of them, gorillas and chimpanzees. They helped our guards unload the carts. We were taken out of the cages one by one, stuffed into big sacks, and carried inside the building. I put up no resistance and let myself be hauled off by two gorillas dressed in white. For several minutes I had the feeling that we were going down some long corridors and climbing some staircases. Eventually I was dumped down on the ground; then, after the sack had been opened, I was thrown into another cage, this time a stationary one, its floor covered with straw. I was alone. One of the gorillas carefully locked the door from the outside.

The room in which I found myself contained a large number of cages like mine, lined up in two rows and facing a long passage. Most of them were already occupied, some of them by my companions of the roundup who had just been brought here, others by men and women who must have been captured some time earlier. The latter could be recognized by their attitude of resignation. They looked at the newcomers with a listless air, scarcely pricking up their ears when one of them gave a plaintive moan. I also noticed that the newcomers had been placed, as I had, in individual cells, whereas the old hands were generally locked up in pairs. Putting my nose through the bars, I saw a bigger cage at the end of the corridor containing a large number of children. Unlike the adults, these appeared to be extremely excited by the arrival of our batch. They gesticulated, jostled one another, and pretended to shake the bars, uttering little cries like young monkeys quarreling.

The two gorillas came back carrying another sack. My friend Nova emerged from it, and again I had the consolation of seeing her put into the cage directly across from mine. She protested this operation in her own way, trying to scratch and bite. When the door was closed on her, she rushed to the bars, tried to break them down, grinding her teeth and whimpering enough to rend one's heart. After a few minutes of this behavior she caught sight of me, stood stock-still, and extended her neck slightly, like a surprised animal. I gave her a cautious half-smile and a little wave, which to my intense delight she clumsily tried to imitate.

I was distracted by the return of the two gorillas in white jackets. The unloading had been completed, for they carried no further bundle, but they pushed in front of them a hand cart laden with food and buckets of water that they dished out to the captives, thus restoring order among them.

It was soon my turn. While one of the gorillas mounted guard, the other entered my cage and placed in front of me a bowl containing some mash, a little fruit, and a bucket. I had decided to do all I could to establish contact with these apes, who seemed to be the only rational and civilized beings on the planet. The one who brought my food did not look unpleasant. Observing my tranquillity, he even gave me a friendly tap on the shoulder. I looked him straight in the eye, then, putting my hand on my chest, gave a ceremonious bow. I saw intense surprise on his face as I raised my head again. I then smiled at him, putting all my heart into this gesture. He was just about to leave; dumfounded, he stopped short and uttered an exclamation. At last I had succeeded in attracting attention to myself. Wishing to reinforce this success by showing all my abilities, I uttered rather stupidly the first phrase that came into my head:

"How do you do? I am a man from Earth. I've had a long journey."

The meaning was unimportant. I only needed to speak in order to reveal my true nature to him. I had certainly achieved my aim. Never before had such stupefaction been seen on an ape's face. He stood breathless and gaping, and so did his companion. They both started talking together in an undertone, but the result was not what I had hoped for. After peering at me suspiciously, the gorilla briskly drew back and stepped out of the cage, which he closed behind him with even greater care than before. The two apes then looked at each other for a moment and began roaring with laughter. I must have represented a truly unique phenomenon, for they could not stop making merry at my expense. Tears were streaming down their faces, and one of them had to put down the bowl he was holding to take out his handkerchief.

My disappointment was such that I immediately

broke into a towering rage. I, too, began shaking the bars, baring my teeth and cursing them in every language I knew. When I had exhausted my repertoire of invectives I went on giving incoherent yells, the only result being that they shrugged their shoulders.

Nevertheless I had succeeded in drawing their attention to me. As they went off, they turned around several times to look back at me. When I had finally calmed down, completely exhausted, I saw one of them take a notebook from his pocket and scribble something in it after carefully recording a sign inscribed on a panel at the top of my cage, which I assumed to be a number.

They disappeared. The other captives, at first agitated by my demonstration, had resumed eating. There was nothing else I could do but eat and rest while waiting for a more favorable opportunity to reveal my noble nature. I gulped down another mash of cereals and some delicious fruit. Opposite me, Nova stopped munching every now and then to dart a furtive glance in my direction.

thirteen

We were left to ourselves for the rest of the day. In the evening, after giving us another meal, the gorillas withdrew, putting out the lights. I slept little that night, not because of the discomfort of the cage—the straw litter was thick and afforded an acceptable bed—but I could not stop working out ways and means to enter into communication with the apes. I resolved never to lose my temper again but to seek patiently and ceaselessly every opportunity to display my mental faculties. The two warders with whom I had dealt were probably lowly underlings incapable of interpreting my movements, but there surely existed other apes who were more civilized.

On the following morning I saw that this hope was not unfounded. I had been awake for an hour.

Most of my companions were restlessly pacing up and down their cages in the manner of captive animals. When I realized I was doing likewise, and had been doing so for some time without noticing it, I was ashamed of myself and forced myself to sit down behind the bars, assuming as human and as pensive an attitude as possible. It was then that the door of the corridor was pushed open and I saw a new figure enter the room accompanied by the two warders. It was a female chimpanzee, and I realized from the way the gorillas kept in the background that she held an important post in the establishment.

The warders must have given her a report about me, for no sooner had she come in than she questioned one of them, who promptly pointed his finger in my direction. Thereupon she came straight over to my cage.

I watched her carefully as she approached. She, too, was dressed in a white smock, cut more elegantly than those worn by the gorillas, gathered in at the waist by a belt and with short sleeves that revealed two agile dangling arms. What struck me most about her was her expression, which was remarkably alert and intelligent. I felt this augured well for our future relationship. She seemed to be quite young in spite of the simian wrinkles that framed her white muzzle. In her hand she carried a leather brief case.

She came to a halt in front of my cage and began

to scrutinize me, at the same time taking a note-book out of her brief case.

"Good day to you, madame," I said with a bow.

I had spoken in my gentlest voice. A look of intense surprise came over the she-ape's face, but she maintained her composure and with a gesture of authority silenced the gorillas, who had started sniggering again.

"Madame or mademoiselle," I went on, feeling encouraged, "I am sorry to present myself to you in these conditions and in this state of undress. Believe me, I'm not in the habit . . ."

I was again spouting whatever nonsense came into my head, selecting only words in keeping with the polite tone I had made up my mind to maintain. When I finished speaking, punctuating my speech with the gentlest of smiles, her surprise changed to stupefaction. Her eyes blinked several times and the wrinkles on her forehead grew more pronounced. It was obvious that she was trying desperately to find the solution to a difficult problem. She in turn smiled at me, and I had the impression that she was beginning to suspect a part of the truth.

During this scene the men in their cages watched us, this time without showing the hatred that the sound of my voice usually provoked in them. They showed signs of curiosity. One after another, they stopped their feverish pacing and came and glued their faces against the bars to see us better. Nova looked furious and could not keep still.

The she-ape took a fountain pen from her pocket and inscribed several lines in her notebook. Then, raising her head and again meeting my anxious gaze, she smiled once more. This encouraged me to make another friendly advance. I stretched an arm out through the bars, keeping my hand open. The gorillas gave a start and made as though to come between us. But the she-ape, whose first reaction had been to draw back, recovered herself, stopped them with one word, and, without taking her eyes off me, likewise stretched out her hairy arm, which trembled a little, toward mine. I did not move. She drew nearer still and placed her hand with its excessively long fingers on my wrist. I felt her tremble at this contact. I did my best not to make any movement that might startle her. She felt my hand, stroked my arm, then turned around to her assistants with an air of triumph.

I was breathless with hope, feeling more and more certain that she was beginning to recognize my noble quality. When she spoke haughtily to one of the gorillas, I was insane enough to hope that my cage was about to be thrown open, with a million apologies. Alas, that was not what happened! The warder fumbled in his pocket and took out a small white object that he handed to his superior. She herself put it in my hand with a charming smile. It was a lump of sugar.

A lump of sugar! I fell from such a height, I suddenly felt so discouraged by the humiliation of this reward, that I almost flung it back in her face. Just in time I remembered my good resolutions and forced myself to remain calm. I took the sugar, bowed, and munched it with as intelligent an air as possible.

Such was my first encounter with Zira. Zira was the she-ape's name, as I presently learned. She was the head of the department to which I had been brought. In spite of my disappointment, her manner gave me some hope and I had a feeling that I would manage to enter into communication with her. She had a long conversation with the warders and I fancied she was giving them instructions about me. Then she continued on her rounds, inspecting the other occupants of the cages.

She carefully scrutinized each of the newcomers and made a few notes, more succinct than in my case. She never ventured to touch one of them. Had she done so, I believe I should have been jealous. I was beginning to feel proud of being the exceptional subject who alone deserved privileged treatment. When I saw her stop in front of the children and throw some sugar to them as well, I felt definitely vexed, certainly no less vexed than Nova, who, after baring her teeth at the she-ape, had lain down in fury at the bottom of her cage with her back turned on me.

fourteen

The second day went by like the first. The apes did not bother about us except to bring us food. I was more and more puzzled about this strange establishment when, on the following day, we were given a series of tests, the memory of which humiliates me even today but which provided some distraction at the time.

The first one struck me at first as rather unusual. One of the warders came up to me while his colleague was working in another cage. My gorilla kept one hand hidden behind his back; in the other he held a whistle. He looked at me to attract my attention, put the whistle to his mouth, and produced a series of shrill blasts: this for a whole minute. Then he held out his other hand, ostentatiously showing me one of those bananas that I had enjoyed and to which all the men appeared to be partial. He held the fruit out in front of me, without taking his eyes off me.

I stretched out my hand, but the banana was out of reach and the gorilla did not come any closer. He looked disappointed and seemed to be expecting another gesture. After a moment he gave up, hid the fruit away again, and resumed his whistling. I was nervous, intrigued by this play-acting, and I almost lost patience when he once more waved the fruit out of reach. I managed to stay calm, however, trying to guess what was being expected of me, for he looked more and more surprised, as though confronted with behavior that was abnormal. He went through the same motions five or six times, then moved along to another captive.

I had a distinct feeling of frustration when I saw that this captive was given the banana at the very first trial, and so was the next one. I closely watched the other gorilla, who was going through the same ceremony with the row opposite. Since he was now dealing with Nova, I did not miss one of her reactions. He whistled, then brandished the fruit as his colleague had done. Immediately the young girl became excited, moving her jaws and . . .

All of a sudden I understood. Nova, the gorgeous Nova, had started watering at the mouth at the sight of this titbit, like a dog when it is offered a lump of sugar. That was what the gorilla was waiting for, as far as this day was concerned. He let her have the desired object and went on to another cage.

I had understood, I tell you, and I was not very proud of it! I had studied biology at one time, and Pavlov's work held no secrets for me. Here they were, applying to men the very experiments he had carried out on dogs. And I, who had been so stupid a few minutes before, now, with my rational brain and education, not only grasped the nature of this test but also foresaw those that were to follow. For several days, perhaps, the monkeys would operate in this manner: blasts on a whistle, then the offer of a favorite food, the latter causing the subject's mouth to water. After a certain period it would be the sound of the whistle alone that would produce the effect. The men would have acquired what are known in scientific jargon as conditioned reflexes.

I could not stop congratulating myself on my perspicacity and could hardly wait to put it to good use. As my gorilla walked past me again, having finished his rounds, I tried by every means to attract his attention. I tapped on the bars; I made sweeping gestures, pointing at my mouth, with the result that he condescended to resume the experiment. Then, at the first blast of the whistle, and well before he had waved the fruit, I started watering at the mouth, watering at the mouth in fury, in frenzy—I, Ulysse Mérou, started watering at the mouth as though my very life depended on it, such pleasure did I derive from showing him my intelligence.

As a matter of fact he appeared extremely dismayed, called his colleague over, and had a long talk with him, as on the previous day. I could follow the elementary reasoning of these clodhoppers: here was a man who only a moment before had no reflexes at all and who suddenly has acquired conditioned reflexes, which required a long time and considerable patience in the case of the others! I felt pity for the weakness of their intellect, which prevented them from discerning the only possible cause for this sudden progress: the capacity for thought. I am sure Zira would have been brighter.

Yet my skill and excess of zeal had a very different result from what I had expected. They went away without giving me the fruit, which one of them started munching himself. There was no longer any point in rewarding me, since the desired end had been achieved without it.

They came back the following day with other equipment. One of them was carrying a bell; the other trundled before him a machine that bore a close resemblance to an electric generator. This time, prepared for the kind of experiment to which we were to be subjected, I understood what they planned to do with these instruments even before they were put into action.

They began with Nova's neighbor, a big strapping fellow with a particularly dull expression who had come up to the edge of his cage and was clutching the bars as we all did nowadays at our jailers' approach. One of the gorillas started swinging the bell, which gave out a solemn ring, while the other connected the generator to the bars of the cage. When the bell had sounded for some time, the second operator started turning the handle of the machine. The man leaped backward, uttering a plaintive cry.

They went through this business several times on the same subject, who was coaxed by the offer of some fruit to come back and cling to the bars. The object, I knew, was to make him leap backward at the sound of the bell and before the electric shock (yet another conditioned reflex), but it was not achieved that day, the man's faculties not being sufficiently developed to enable him to relate cause and effect.

I waited for them, on the other hand, chuckling to myself, eager to show them the difference between instinct and intelligence. At the first sound of the bell I let go of the bars and retreated to the middle of the cage. At the same time I looked at them and gave a mocking smile. The gorillas wrinkled their brows. They no longer laughed at my behavior and for the first time appeared to suspect that I was teasing them.

They had decided nevertheless to do the experiment over a second time, when their attention was diverted by the arrival of some new visitors.

fifteen

Three figures were coming down the passage: Zira, the female chimpanzee, and two other apes, one of whom was plainly in a high position.

He was an orangutan, the first I had seen on the planet Soror. He was shorter than the gorillas and slightly round-shouldered. His arms were relatively longer so that he often touched the ground with his hands as he walked, which the other apes did only rarely. He thus gave me the odd impression of using a couple of walking sticks. His head adorned with long coarse hair and sunk between his shoulders, his face frozen in an expression of pedantic meditation, he looked like a venerable and solemn old pontiff. He was also dressed quite differently from the others, in a long black frock coat with a red star in the buttonhole and black-and-white-striped trousers, both somewhat dusty.

He was followed by a little female chimpanzee carrying a heavy brief case. Her attitude suggested that she was his secretary. By this time no one is surprised, I imagine, by my repeated reference to significant attitudes and expressions among these apes. I am convinced that any rational being confronted with this couple would have concluded, as I did, that the one was a learned elder and the other his humble secretary. Their arrival gave me an opportunity of noting again the sense of hierarchy that seemed to exist among the apes. Zira showed every sign of respect for this superior of hers. The two gorillas went forward to meet him as soon as they caught sight of him and bowed low before him. The orangutan gave a condescending little wave of his hand.

They made straight for my cage. Was I not the most interesting subject of the lot? I welcomed the great authority with my most affable smile and addressed him in ringing tones:

"My dear orangutan, how happy I am to find myself at last in the presence of a creature who exhales wisdom and intelligence! I am sure we are going to understand each other, you and I."

The old dear had given a start at the sound of my voice. He scratched his ear for some time and peered suspiciously into my cage as though scenting some trickery. Zira then addressed him, notebook in hand, reading out the particulars she had jotted down about me. She did her best, but it was plain to see that the orangutan refused to be convinced. He uttered two or three sentences in a pompous manner, shrugged his shoulders several times, shook his head, then put his hands behind his back and started pacing up and down the corridor, passing and repassing my cage and darting glances in my direction that were far from kindly. The other apes waited for his decision in respectful silence.

In seemingly respectful silence, at least—for their respect appeared far from genuine when I intercepted a furtive sign from one gorilla to the other, the sense of which allowed no room for doubt: they were making fun of the boss behind his back. This, combined with the annoyance I felt at his attitude toward me, inspired me with the idea of putting on a little act designed to convince him of my mental ability. I started pacing to and fro in the cage, imitating his gait, my shoulders hunched, my hands behind my back, my brow wrinkled in an air of profound meditation.

The gorillas choked with laughter and Zira herself was unable to keep a straight face. As for the secretary, she was obliged to plunge her muzzle into her brief case to hide her amusement. I was congratulating myself on my demonstration when I suddenly realized it was dangerous. Noticing my mimicry, the orangutan looked very annoyed and in a dry voice uttered a few sharp words that restored order immediately. Then he stopped in front of me and started dictating his notes to his secretary.

He went on dictating for a long time, punctuating his phrases with pompous gestures. I was beginning to have enough of his blindness and resolved to give him fresh proof of my capacities. Stretching my arms out toward him, I spoke up to the best of my ability:

"Mi Zaius."

I had noticed that all the underlings who addressed him began with these two words. Zaius, I subsequently learned, was the pontiff's name, "mi" an honorific title.

The monkeys were flabbergasted. They no longer wanted to laugh, least of all Zira, who seemed extremely perturbed, especially when I pointed a finger at her and added "Zira," a name I had also remembered and that could only be hers. As for Zaius, he was completely flustered and started pacing up and down the corridor again, shaking his head with an air of incredulity.

Having finally recovered his composure, he gave orders for me to be subjected in his presence to the tests I had been given the previous day. I acquitted myself well. I watered at the mouth at the first blast of the whistle. I leaped back at the sound of the bell. He made me repeat this last operation a dozen times, dictating countless comments to his secretary.

In the end I had an inspiration. At the moment the gorilla began to ring the bell, I unfastened the clip that connected the electric wire to my cage and threw the cable outside. Then I held on to the bars and stayed where I was, while the other warder, who had not noticed my trick, struggled to turn the handle of the now harmless generator.

I was very proud of this move, which was bound to be irrefutable proof of wisdom to any rational creature. In fact, Zira's attitude showed me that she, at least, was extremely impressed. She looked at me with singular intensity and her white muzzle turned pink—which, as I learned later, is a sign of emotion in chimpanzees. But there was nothing I could do to convince the orangutan. This fiendish ape again started shrugging his shoulders nastily and shaking his head energetically when Zira spoke to him. He was a methodical scientist; he refused to listen to such nonsense. He gave further instructions to the gorillas and I was given another test, a combination of the first two.

I knew this one, too. I had seen it practiced on dogs in certain laboratories. The idea was to bewilder the subject, to provoke a mental confusion by combining two reactions. One of the gorillas emitted a series of blasts on his whistle as the promise of a reward, while the other rang the bell that announced a punishment. I recalled the conclusions of a noted biologist concerning a similar experiment: it was possible, he said, by so abusing an animal, to produce in him emotional disorders strangely reminiscent of neurosis in men, and sometimes even to send him out of his mind by repeating these maneuvers fairly often.

I took care not to fall into the trap: but, clearly pricking up my ears at the sound of the whistle, then at that of the bell, I sat down halfway between the two, my chin resting in my hand, in the traditional attitude of the thinker. Zira could not help clapping her hands. Zaius took a handkerchief out of his pocket and mopped his brow.

He was sweating, but nothing could shake his stupid skepticism. This I could see from his expression after a vehement discussion he had with the she-ape. He dictated some more notes to his secretary, gave some detailed instructions to Zira, who listened to them with a far from satisfied air, and finally went off after darting another churlish glance at me.

Zira spoke to the gorillas and I quickly realized she was giving them orders to leave me in peace, at least for the rest of the day, for they went off with their equipment. Then she came back to my cage by herself and observed me again, in silence, for a long time. After which, of her own accord, she stretched out her hand in a friendly gesture. I seized it with emotion, meanwhile gently whispering her name. The blush that mantled her muzzle showed me she was deeply touched.

sixteen

Zaius came back a few days later, and his visit was the signal for a complete reorganization of the room. But I must first describe how I had meanwhile distinguished myself still further in the eyes of the apes.

The day after the orangutan's first inspection an avalanche of new tests descended upon us, the first at mealtimes. Instead of putting our food in the cages as they usually did, Zoram and Zanam, the two gorillas whose names I had finally learned, hoisted them to the ceiling in baskets by means of a system of pulleys with which the cages were equipped. At the same time they placed four fairly big wooden cubes in each cell. Then, stepping back, they observed us.

It was heart-rending to see my companions' discomfort. They tried to jump, but none of them could reach the basket. Some climbed up the bars but, having reached the top, they stretched out their arms in vain since they could not get hold of the food, which was some distance away from the sides of the cages. I was ashamed at the stupidity of these men. I, needless to say, had found the solution to the problem immediately. One merely had to pile the four cubes one on top of another, then climb onto this scaffolding and unhook the basket. This is what I did, with an air of detachment that concealed my pride. It was not a stroke of genius, but I was the only one to show myself so skillful. Zoram and Zanam's obvious admiration went straight to my heart.

I started to eat, without concealing my contempt for the other captives, who were incapable of following my example even after having watched the maneuver. Nova herself could not imitate me that day, although I repeated the action several times for her benefit. She did try, however—she was certainly one of the most intelligent of the lot—she tried to pile one cube on another, but she placed it crookedly so that it overbalanced; then, terrified by the crash it made in falling, she took refuge in a corner. This girl, endowed with remarkable suppleness and agility, whose every gesture was graceful, proved to be as hopelessly clumsy as the others when it came to handling an object. She succeeded, however, in mastering the trick within two days.

That morning I took pity on her and threw her

two of the best bits of fruit through the bars. This gesture earned me a caress from Zira, who had just come in. I allowed myself to be stroked by her hairy hand, much to the displeasure of Nova, whom these demonstrations enraged and who forthwith started jumping up and down and whimpering.

I distinguished myself in many other tests; but above all, by listening carefully, I managed to retain a few simple words of the simian language and to understand their meaning. I practiced pronouncing them whenever Zira went past my cage, and she looked more and more astounded. I had reached this stage when Zaius' new inspection took place.

Once again he was escorted by his secretary, but accompanied also by another orangutan as solemn as he and wearing the same decoration, and who chatted with him on an equal footing. I assumed he was a colleague who had been called into consultation over the disturbing case that I represented. They started a long discussion in front of my cage with Zira, who had meanwhile joined them. The she-ape spoke at great length and with fervor. I knew she was trying to plead my cause, pointing out the exceptional keenness of my intelligence, which no longer could be contested. But the only result of her intervention was to provoke an incredulous smile from the two scientists.

I was once again required to undergo the tests at which I had proved so adroit. The last one consisted in opening a box that was closed by nine different systems (bolt, pin, key, hook, etc.). Someone on Earth—Kinnaman, I think it was—had invented a similar device to assess the discernment of monkeys, and this problem was the most complicated any of them had succeeded in solving. The same no doubt applied here in the case of men. I had acquitted myself with honor after the first few attempts.

Zira herself handed me the box, and I saw from her air of entreaty that she was fervently hoping to see me perform brilliantly, as though her own reputation was involved in the test. I did my best to satisfy her and operated the nine mechanisms in a flash, without a moment's hesitation. Nor did I confine myself to that. I took out the fruit that the box contained and gallantly offered it to her. She accepted with a blush. Then I revealed my major achievement and pronounced the few words I had mastered, pointing out the objects to which they corresponded.

This time I felt it was impossible that they could entertain further doubt as to my true condition. Alas, I did not yet know the blindness of orangutans! They again gave that skeptical smile that enraged me so much, paid no attention to Zira, and went on with their discussion. They had listened to me as though I were a parrot. I felt they were only prepared to attribute my talents to a sort of instinct and a keen sense of mimicry. They had probably adopted the scientific rule that one of our learned men at home summarized as follows: "In no case may we interpret an action as the outcome of the exercise of a higher psychical faculty if it can be interpreted as the outcome of one that stands lower in the psychological scale."

Such was the obvious meaning of their jargon, and I began fuming with rage. No doubt I should have yielded to some angry outburst had I not intercepted a glance from Zira. It was plain to see that she did not agree with them and felt ashamed to hear them talking like this in front of me.

His colleague having eventually gone off, doubtless after pronouncing a categorical opinion on my case, Zaius embarked on some other exercises. He did the rounds of the hall, examining each of the captives in turn and giving fresh instructions to Zira, who noted them down. His movements seemed to indicate numerous changes in the occupancy of the cages. It did not take me long to discover his plan and to understand the purpose of the evident comparisons he was making between certain characteristics and such-and-such man and those of such-and-such woman.

I was not mistaken. The gorillas were now carrying out the boss's orders, which Zira had passed on to them. We were redistributed in couples. What fiendish tests were indicated by this pairing off? What peculiarities of the human race did these apes, with their mania for experiments, wish to study? My acquaintance with biological laboratories had suggested the answer to me: to a scientist who has chosen instinct and reflexes as his field of study, the sexual instinct has an exceptional interest.

That was it! These demons wanted to use us—to use me, who found myself attached to this herd by an extravagant whim of fate—to study in captivity the amorous practices of men, the methods of approach of the male and the female, the manner in which they copulate, in order to compare them perhaps with earlier observations of the same men in the wild state. Doubtless they also intended to experiment with sexual selectivity?

As soon as I understood their plan, I felt more humiliated than I had ever been in my life and swore to die rather than lend myself to these degrading schemes. Yet my shame was substantially reduced, I must admit, although my resolution was still firm, when I saw the woman whom science had assigned as my mate. It was Nova. I felt almost inclined to forgive the old pedant his stupidity and blindness, and I made no protest when Zoram and Zanam seized me around the waist and flung me at the feet of the nymph of the torrent.

seventeen

I shall not give a detailed account of the scenes that took place in the cages during the weeks that followed. As I had guessed, the apes had taken it into their heads to study the amorous behavior of humans, and they tackled this task in their usual methodical manner, noting the slightest developments, struggling to provoke relationships, making use of their pikes now and then to correct a recalcitrant subject's conduct.

I had begun to make a few observations myself, hoping to include them in the account I intended publishing on my eventual return to Earth, but I soon grew tired of this, finding nothing very intriguing to note—nothing, that is, apart from the strange manner in which each man courted his

woman before approaching her. He indulged in a
display similar in every way to that executed by
certain birds: a sort of slow, hesitant dance consisting of steps forward, backward, and sideways.
He moved thus in an ever-decreasing circle, a circle
whose center was occupied by the woman, who
merely pivoted around without shifting from her
position. I witnessed with interest several of these
displays, the essential ritual of which was always
the same, the details varying only occasionally. As
for the copulation that concluded these prelimi-
naries, even though I was slightly astonished when I
first witnessed it, I soon ended up by paying no
more attention to it than the rest of the captives.
The only surprising element in these displays was
the scientific ardor with which the apes followed
them, never omitting to make copious notes on the
procedure.

It was a different matter when, noticing I did not
indulge in these frolics—I had sworn that nothing
would induce me to make such an exhibition of
myself—the gorillas took it into their heads to compel
me by force and to belabor me with their pikes—
me, Ulysse Mérou, a man created in the image of
God! I resisted them energetically. These brutes persisted and I don't know what would have become of
me had it not been for the arrival of Zira, to whom
they reported my lack of cooperation.

She pondered for a long time; then, looking at me
with her fine intelligent eyes, came up and started

stroking the back of my neck, meanwhile addressing me in terms that I assumed to signify something like this:

"Poor little man," she seemed to be saying. "How odd you are! No one of your species has ever behaved like this before. Look at the others all around you. Do what you have been asked to do and you will be rewarded."

She took a lump of sugar out of her pocket and offered it to me. I was in despair. So she too regarded me as an animal, perhaps a slightly more intelligent one than the others. I shook my head furiously and went and lay down in the corner of the cage, far from Nova, who gazed at me in incomprehension.

That would doubtless have been the end of the business had not Zaius reappeared at that moment, looking more overbearing than ever. He had come to see the outcome of his experiments and as usual he inquired first about me. Zira was obliged to tell him of my recalcitrance. He seemed extremely displeased, paced up and down for a minute or two with his hands behind his back, then gave some decisive orders. Zoram and Zanam opened my cage, took Nova away from me, and brought back instead an elderly matron. That idiot Zaius, steeped in scientific method, was determined to try the same experiment with a different subject.

Worse was to come, however, and I did not even think of my own sad fate. In anguish I watched my friend Nova being bundled off and was horrified to see her put into the cage directly opposite, delivered to a man with hefty shoulders, a sort of hair-chested colossus, who started dancing around her, embarking with frenzied ardor on the curious love display I have already described.

As soon as I saw what this brute was up to, I forgot my good resolutions. I lost my head and once again behaved like a madman. As a matter of fact, I was literally mad with rage. I screamed and yelled like the men of Soror, showing my fury as they did by hurling myself against the bars, biting them, foaming at the mouth, grinding my teeth, behaving in short in a thoroughly bestial fashion.

And the most surprising thing about this outburst was its unexpected outcome. Seeing me behave like this, Zaius smiled. It was the first mark of benevolence he had bestowed on me. He had finally detected in me human behavior and found himself on familiar ground. His theory was vindicated. This put him in such a good mood that he even consented, at a remark from Zira, to cancel his orders and give me one last chance. The dreadful old matron was led away and Nova was restored to me before the hefty brute had touched her. The group of monkeys then stood back and all three watched me closely from a distance.

What more can I say? These emotions had broken down my resistance. I felt I would never be able to bear the sight of my nymph at the mercy of another man. I resigned myself like a coward to the victory of the orangutan, who was now smiling with pleasure at his astuteness. Hesitantly I attempted a step of the dance.

Yes, I, one of the kings of creation, started circling around my beauty—I, the ultimate achievement of millennial evolution, in front of this collection of apes eagerly watching me, in front of an old orangutan dictating notes to his secretary, in front of a female chimpanzee smiling with self-satisfaction, in front of a couple of chuckling gorillas—I, a man, excusing myself on the grounds of exceptional cosmic circumstances, and persuading myself for the moment that there are more things on the planets and in the heavens than have ever been dreamed of in human philosophy, I, Ulysse Mérou, embarked like a peacock around the gorgeous Nova on the love display.

TWO

eighteen

I must now admit that I adapted myself with remarkable ease to the conditions of life in my cage.
From the material point of view, I was living in perfect felicity: during the day the apes attended to
my every need; at night I shared my litter with one
of the loveliest girls in the cosmos. I even grew
so accustomed to this situation that for more than
a month, without feeling how outlandish or degrading it was, I made no attempt to put an end to
it. I learned hardly any new words of the simian
language. I did not continue with my attempts to
enter into communication with Zira, so that the
latter, if she had once had an inkling as to my spiritual nature, had no doubt since yielded to Zaius'
opinion and regarded me as a man of her planet,

that is, an animal: an intelligent animal, perhaps, but by no means an intellectual one.

My superiority over the other prisoners, which I no longer exercised to the point of startling the warders, made me the most brilliant subject in the establishment. This distinction, I am ashamed to admit, sufficed my present ambitions and even filled me with pride. Zoram and Zanam were friendly toward me, taking pleasure in seeing me smile, laugh, and pronounce a few words. Having exhausted all the classic tests with me, they racked their brains to invent other, more subtle ones, and all three of us made merry whenever I discovered the solution to a problem. They never forgot to bring me some titbit, which I always shared with Nova. We were a privileged couple. I was fatuous enough to believe that my mate was aware of all she owed to my talents, and I spent part of my time showing off in front of her.

One day, however, after several weeks, I felt a sort of nausea. Was it the gleam in Nova's eyes, which had seemed to me that night particularly lacking in expression? Was it the lump of sugar that Zira came to give me that suddenly acquired a bitter taste? The fact is that I was shamed by my cowardly resignation. What would Professor Antelle think of me, if he chanced to be still alive and found me in this state? This thought soon became unbearable, and I forthwith made up my mind to behave like a civilized man.

While stroking Zira's arm by way of expressing

my thanks, I snatched away her notebook and fountain pen. I braved her gentle remonstrances, sat down on the straw, and started a drawing of Nova. I am a fairly good draftsman and, being inspired by the model, managed to turn out a reasonable likeness, which I then handed to the she-ape.

This promptly reawakened her emotion and uncertainty about me. Her muzzle became red and she peered at me closely, trembling slightly. Since she made no further move, I again calmly seized her notebook, which this time she yielded to me without protest. Why had I not thought of this simple solution before? Mustering my school-day memories, I drew the geometrical figure illustrating the theorem of Pythagoras. It was not at random that I chose this proposition: I remembered reading in my youth a prophetic book in which such a procedure had been used by an old scientist to enter into communication with the spirits of another world. I had even discussed this during the voyage with Professor Antelle, who approved of the method. He had added, I distinctly remembered, that the Euclidean rules, being completely false, were no doubt for that very reason universal.

In any case, the effect it had on Zira was extraordinary. Her muzzle went purple and she gave a sharp exclamation. She did not recover her composure until Zoram and Zanam came up, intrigued by her attitude. Then she reacted in a way that I found extremely odd—after darting a furtive glance at me, she carefully hid the drawing I had just completed. She spoke to the gorillas, who then left the hall, and I realized she had sent them off on some pretext or other. Then she turned back to me and took my hand, the pressure of her fingers having quite a different significance from when she flattered me like a young animal after a successful trick. Finally she handed me the notebook and fountain pen with an air of entreaty.

Now it was she who appeared eager to establish contact. I gave thanks to Pythagoras and embarked once more on my geometry. On one page of the notebook I drew to the best of my ability the three conic sections with their axes and centers: an ellipse, a parabola, and an hyperbola. Then, on the opposite page, I drew a right circular cone. Let me remind the reader that the intersection of such a body by a plane produces one of the three conic sections, depending on the angle of the cut. In this case I drew the figure to illustrate an ellipse, then, reverting to my first diagram, pointed out the corresponding curve to my astonished she-ape.

She snatched the notebook out of my hands and in turn drew another cone, intersected at a different angle, and pointed out the hyperbola with her long finger. I felt such intense emotion that tears came to my eyes and I clasped her hands convulsively. Nova whimpered with rage at the far end of the cage. Her instinct did not deceive her as to the meaning of these demonstrations. It was a spiritual communion that had just been established between Zira and me through the medium of geometry. I derived an almost sensual satisfaction from this and felt that the she-ape was also deeply moved.

She broke free with a sudden jerk and rushed from the hall. She was absent only a few minutes, but during this time I remained lost in thought without daring to look at Nova, about whom I felt almost guilty and who turned her back on me with a growl.

When Zira came back she handed me a large sheet of paper fixed to a drawing board. I thought for a second or two and made up my mind to deliver a decisive blow. In one corner of the sheet I sketched the system of Betelgeuse, as we had discovered it on our arrival, with the giant central body and its four planets. I marked Soror down in its exact position together with its own little satellite; I indicated it to Zira, then pointed my forefinger at her repeatedly. She signaled to me that she had understood completely.

Then in another corner of the sheet I drew our dear old solar system with its principal planets. I indicated the Earth and pointed my finger at my own chest.

This time Zira was slower to understand. She, too, indicated the Earth, then pointed her finger upward. I gave an affirmative nod. She was flabbergasted and her mental turmoil was plain to see. I did my best to help her by drawing another dotted line between Earth and Soror and marking in our vessel, on a different scale, on the trajectory. This made her see the light. I was now certain that my true nature and origin were known to her. She was about to draw closer to me but at that moment Zaius appeared at the end of the corridor for his periodical inspection.

A look of terror came into the she-ape's eyes. She quickly crumpled up the paper, put her notebook back in her pocket, and, before the orangutan had reached us, placed her forefinger on her mouth with an air of entreaty. She was counseling me not to show myself in my true colors to Zaius. I obeyed her without understanding the reason for these mysteries and, convinced that I had an ally in her, promptly resumed my intelligent animal attitude.

nineteen

From then on, thanks to Zira, my knowledge of the simian world and language increased rapidly. She contrived to see me alone almost every day on the pretext of some test and undertook my education, instructing me in the language and at the same time learning mine with a rapidity that amazed me. In less than two months we were capable of holding a conversation on a variety of subjects. Little by little I came to understand the planet Soror, and it is the characteristics of this strange civilization that I am now going to try to describe.

As soon as we could converse together, Zira and I, I directed the conversation toward the principal object of my curiosity: Were the apes the only rational beings, the kings of creation on the planet?

"What do you think?" she said. "Ape is of course the only rational creature, the only one possessing a mind as well as a body. The most materialistic of our scientists recognize the supernatural essence of the simian mind."

Phrases like this always gave me a start in spite of myself.

"Well then, Zira, what are men?"

We were then speaking French, for, as I have said, she was quicker to learn my language than I hers. At the outset there were some difficulties of interpretation, the words "man" and "ape" not evoking the same creatures for us; but this snag was quickly smoothed out. Each time she said "ape," I mentally translated "superior being, the height of evolution." When she spoke about men, I knew she meant bestial creatures endowed with a certain sense of imitation and presenting a few anatomical similarities to apes but of an embryonic psyche and devoid of the power of thought.

"It was only a century ago," she said dogmatically, "that we made some remarkable progress in the science of origins. It used to be thought that species were immutable, created with their present characteristics by an all-powerful God. But a line of great thinkers, all of them chimpanzees, have modified our ideas on this subject completely. Today we know that all species are mutable and probably have a common source."

"So that apes probably descend from men?"

"Some of us thought so; but it is not exactly that. Apes and men are two separate branches that have evolved from a point in common but in different directions, the former gradually developing to the stage of rational thought, the others stagnating in their animal state. Many orangutans, however, still insist on denying this obvious fact."

"You were saying Zira . . . a line of great thinkers, all of them chimpanzees?"

I am reporting these conversations as they occurred, in non-consecutive snatches, my eagerness to learn leading Zira into countless lengthy digressions.

"Almost all the great discoveries," she stated vehemently, "have been made by chimpanzees."

"Are there different classes among the apes?"

"There are three distinct families, as you have noticed, each of which has its own characteristics: chimpanzees, gorillas, and orangutans. The racial barriers that used to exist have been abolished and the disputes arising from them have been settled, thanks mainly to the campaigns launched by the chimpanzees. Today, in principle, there is no difference at all between us."

"But most of the great discoveries," I persisted, "were made by the chimpanzees."

"That is true."

"What about the gorillas?"

"They are meat eaters," she said scornfully. "They were overlords and many of them have preserved a lust for power. They enjoy organizing and directing. They love hunting and life in the open air. The poorest of them are engaged on work that requires physical strength."

"And the orangutans?"

Zira looked at me for a moment, then burst out laughing.

"They are Official Science," she said. "You must have noticed this already and you'll have plenty of opportunities to confirm it. They learn an enormous amount from books. They are all decorated. Some of them are looked upon as leading lights in a narrow specialized field that requires a good memory. Apart from that . . ."

She made a gesture of contempt. I did not pursue this subject, but made a mental note to come back to it later. I led the conversation to more general ideas. At my request she drew the genealogical tree of the ape, in so far as the best specialist had determined it. This bore a close resemblance to the diagrams that with us represent the evolutionary process. From a single trunk, whose roots faded away at the base into the unknown, various limbs branched out in succession: vegetables, unicellular organisms, then coelenterata and echinoderms; higher up one arrived at fish, reptiles, and finally mammals. The tree was extended to include a class analogous to our anthropoids, and at this point a new limb branched out: that of men. This branch stopped short, whereas the central stem went on rising, giving birth to different species of prehistoric apes with barbaric names, to culminate eventually in *Simius sapiens*, forming the three extreme points of evolution: the chimpanzee, the gorilla, and the orangutan. It was absolutely clear.

"Ape's brain," Zira concluded, "has developed, is complex and organized, whereas man's has hardly undergone any transformation."

"And why, Zira, has the simian brain developed in this way?"

Language had undoubtedly been an essential factor. But why did apes talk and not men? Scientific opinion differed on this point. There were some who saw in it a mysterious divine intervention. Others maintained that ape's mind was primarily the result of the fact that he had four agile hands.

"With only two hands, each with short, clumsy fingers," said Zira, "man is probably handicapped at birth, incapable of progressing and acquiring a precise knowledge of the universe. Because of this he has never been able to use a tool with any success. Oh, it's possible that he once tried, clumsily. . . . Some curious vestiges have been found. There are a number of research projects going on at this moment into that particular subject. If you're interested in these questions, I'll introduce you someday to Cornelius. He is much more qualified than I am to discuss them."

"Cornelius?"

"My fiancé," said Zira, blushing. "A very great, a real scientist."

"A chimpanzee?"

"Of course. . . . Anyway," she concluded, "that's what I think, too: our being equipped with four hands is one of the most important factors in our spiritual evolution. It helped us in the first place to climb trees, and thereby conceive the three dimensions of space, whereas man, pegged to the ground by a physical malformation, slumbered on the flat. A taste for tools came to us next because we had the potentiality of using them with dexterity. Achievement followed, and it is thus we have raised ourselves to the level of wisdom."

On Earth I had frequently heard precisely the opposite argument used to explain the superiority of man. After thinking it over, however, Zira's reasoning struck me as being neither more nor less convincing than ours.

I should have liked to pursue this conversation, and I still had a thousand questions to ask, when we were interrupted by Zoram and Zanam bringing the evening meal. Zira bade me a hasty good night and went off.

I remained in my cage with Nova as my only companion. We had finished eating. The gorillas had left, after putting out the lights, except the one over the entrance which gave a feeble gleam. I looked at Nova and thought about what I had learned during the day. It was obvious that she did not care for Zira and was vexed by these conversations. At first she had even protested in her usual manner and tried to come between Zira and me, leaping about the cage, tearing up handfuls of straw, and flinging them in the intruder's face. I had had to resort to force to keep her quiet. After receiving a few thundering slaps across her beautiful face, she had eventually calmed down. I had allowed myself to indulge in this brutal behavior almost without thinking; afterward I felt sorry, but she appeared not to hold it against me.

The intellectual effort I had made to assimilate the simian theories of evolution left me worn out. I was happy when I saw Nova creep over to me in the dark and in her usual fashion beg for the half-human, half-animal caresses for which we had gradually worked out the code: a singular code, the details of which are of little importance, composed of compromise and reciprocal concessions to the manners of the civilized world and to the customs of this outlandish human race that populated the planet Soror.

twenty

It was a red-letter day for me. Yielding to my entreaties, Zira had agreed to take me out of the Institute for Advanced Biological Study—that was the name of the establishment—and show me around the town.

She had consented to this only after much hesitation. It had taken me some time to convince her finally of my origin. Until then, though admitting the evidence while in my company, she would later begin doubting again. I tried to put myself in her place. She could only be profoundly shocked by my description of the men and above all of the apes on our Earth. She subsequently told me that for a long time she had preferred to regard me as a sorcerer or a charlatan rather than accept my statements. Yet, confronted with the facts and the evidence I accumulated, she eventually had complete confidence in me and even began to work out a plan to enable me to recover my liberty, which was not easy, as she explained to me that day. Meanwhile she came to fetch me at the beginning of the afternoon to go on our outing.

I felt my heart thumping at the thought of being in the open air again. My enthusiasm was slightly curbed when I saw she was going to keep me on a lead. The gorillas took me out of the cage, banged the door shut in Nova's face, and put around my neck a leather collar to which a strong chain was fixed. Zira took the other end and led me off, while a heart-rending whine from Nova stirred my compassion. But when I showed her a little pity and gave her a friendly wave, Zira looked angry and tugged me forward by the neck. Since she was now convinced I had an ape's mind, my intimacy with the young girl vexed and shocked her.

Her bad temper evaporated when we were alone together in the dark, deserted corridor.

"I don't suppose," she laughed, "that men on Earth are used to being held on a lead like this by apes?"

I assured her they were not at all used to it. She apologized, explaining that even though there were a few tame men who could be taken out like this without causing a scene, it was more normal if I was tied up. Subsequently, if I proved harmless, she might possibly be able to relieve me of my fetters.

And partly forgetting my true condition, as she still often did, she began advising me about my behavior, which humiliated me deeply.

"Above all, do be careful not to turn on passersby or bare your teeth or scratch a trustful child who might come up and pet you. I didn't want to muzzle you, but . . ."

She stopped short and burst out laughing.

"Forgive me, forgive me," she cried. "I keep forgetting you have a mind like an ape."

She gave me a friendly tap on the shoulder by way of apology. Her high spirits dissolved any mounting resentment. I liked to hear her laugh. Nova's inability to manifest her joy in this way sometimes made me sigh. I shared the she-ape's gaiety. In the half-light of the corridor I could no longer see her face except for the tip of her white muzzle. She had put on a smart coat and skirt to go out and a scarf that concealed her ears. For a moment I forgot her simian condition and took her arm. She found my gesture quite natural and did not object. We walked along for a bit like this, side by side. At the end of the corridor, lit by a window in the side wall, she quickly withdrew her arm and pushed me away. Reverting to a more serious mood, she tugged on my chain.

"You mustn't behave like this," she said, looking

slightly distressed. "In the first place, I'm engaged and—"

"You're engaged!"

The incongruity of her remark about my gesture of familiarity struck her at the same time as it did me. She corrected herself, blushing at the muzzle. "I mean, no one must suspect your nature for the moment. It's in your own interests, I assure you."

I took her advice and allowed myself to be led along quietly. We left the building. The porter of the institute, a big gorilla clad in a uniform, let us out, observing me with curiosity after having saluted Zira. On the sidewalk I staggered slightly, giddy from the exercise and dazzled by the glare of Betelgeuse after more than three months' captivity. I inhaled the warm air deeply; at the same time I felt embarrassed to be walking around naked. I had grown used to this in my cage, but here I felt grotesque and indecent under the eyes of the apes passing by, who kept staring at me. Zira had categorically refused to let me wear clothes, maintaining that I would have looked even more ridiculous dressed up, like one of those tame men who are exhibited at fairs. She was no doubt right. In fact, if the passers-by turned around to stare at me, it was not because I was naked but simply because I was a man, a species that in the streets roused the same sort of curiosity as would a chimpanzee in a French city. The adults merely grinned and continued on their way, but some young apes began to gather around me in great glee. Zira quickly led me off toward her car, motioned me into the back seat, sat down herself behind the steering wheel, and drove me slowly along the streets.

The town—the capital of an important simian region—I had barely glimpsed on my arrival, and I now had to resign myself to seeing it peopled by ape pedestrians, ape motorists, ape shopkeepers, ape businessmen, and apes in uniform whose job was to maintain law and order. Apart from this, it did not make a great impression on me. The houses were similar to ours; the roads, which were fairly dirty, looked like our roads. The traffic was less heavy than at home. What struck me most of all was the way the pedestrians crossed the street. There were no marked crossings, only overhead passages consisting of a metal frame to which they clung with all four hands. They all wore fine leather gloves that did not interfere with their prehension.

When she had driven around sufficiently to give me a general picture of the town, Zira stopped her car in front of a tall gate through which I could see banks of flowers.

"The park," she said. "We can go for a little stroll. I should have liked to show you some other things—our museums, for instance, which are outstanding—but that's not possible yet."

I assured her that I should be delighted to stretch my legs.

"And besides," she went on, "we'll be left in peace here. There are not many people about and it's time for us to have a serious conversation."

twenty-one

"I don't think you realize, do you, the danger you are in here on Soror?"

"I've already had some experience of it; but I feel that if I showed myself in my true colors—and I can do so now by providing proof—the apes ought to admit me as their spiritual brother."

"That's where you're wrong. Now listen . . ."

We were strolling through the park. The paths were almost deserted and we had passed no more than one or two courting couples who were roused to a momentary curiosity by my presence. I, on the other hand, stared at them shamelessly, being firmly resolved not to miss a single opportunity to learn about simian customs.

They walked along together holding each other

around the waist, the length of their arms making this embrace a tight and complex encirclement. They would often stop at a corner of a path to exchange a kiss or two. From time to time also, after daring a furtive glance all around, they would take hold of the low branches of a tree and swing themselves off the ground. This they accomplished without separating, each of them using one hand and one foot with an ease that I envied, and they would then disappear into the foliage.

"Now listen," said Zira. "Your launch"—I had told her in detail how we had arrived on the planet—"your launch has been discovered; at least what's left of it after being pillaged. It has aroused the curiosity of our researchers. They realize it was not manufactured here."

"Do you build similar machines?"

"Yes, but not so perfected. From what you've told me, we're a long way behind you. We have, however, already launched artificial satellites around our planet, the last one even being occupied by a living being: a man. We had to destroy it in flight because we were unable to recover it."

"I see," I said, lost in thought. "So men also serve you for this sort of experiment."

"It can't be helped. . . . Anyway, your rocket has been discovered."

"What about our spaceship, which has been in orbit around Soror for the last few months?"

"I haven't heard anything about it. It must have

escaped the notice of our astronomers . . . but do stop interrupting me. Some of our scientists have put forward the theory that the machine comes from another planet and that it was inhabited. They are unable to go a step further and imagine intelligent beings in human form."

"But you must tell them, Zira!" I cried. "I've had enough of living like a prisoner, even in the most comfortable of cages, even looked after by you. Why are you hiding me away? Why not reveal the truth to everyone?"

Zira stopped short, glanced all about her, and put her hand on my arm.

"Why? It's purely in your own interests that I'm doing this. You know Zaius?"

"Of course. I wanted to talk to you about him. Well?"

"Did you notice the effect your first attempts at rationality produced on him? Do you know I've tried a hundred times to tell him about you and to suggest—ever so carefully!—that perhaps you were not a beast in spite of appearances?"

"I've seen you having long conversations together and noticed you didn't agree."

"He's as stubborn as a mule and as stupid as a man!" Zira burst out. "Alas! it's the same with almost all the orangutans. He has decreed once and for all that your talents are due to a highly developed animal instinct, and nothing will make him change his opinion. The unfortunate thing is, he has already prepared a long thesis on you in which he asserts that you are a *tame man*, in other words, a man who has been trained to perform certain tricks without understanding them, probably during a former period of captivity."

"The stupid beast!"

"Certainly. The only snag is, he represents official science and he's powerful. He is one of the highest authorities in the institute, and all my reports have to go through him. I'm almost certain he would accuse me of scientific heresy if I tried to reveal the truth in your case, as you suggest. I should be dismissed. That's unimportant, but do you realize what might then happen to you?"

"What fate could be worse than living in a cage?"

"Be thankful for small mercies! Do you know how I've had to scheme and plot to prevent him from having you transferred to the encephalic section? Nothing could restrain him if you insisted on claiming to be a rational creature."

"What's the encephalic section?" I asked in alarm.

"That's where we perform certain extremely tricky operations on the brain: grafting; observation and alteration of the nervous centers; partial and even total ablation."

"And you carry out these experiments on men!"

"Of course. Man's brain, like the rest of his anatomy, is the one that bears the closest resemblance to ours. It's a lucky chance that nature has put at our disposal an animal on whom we can study our own bodies. Man serves us in many other fields of research, as you'll come to realize. . . . At this very moment we are undertaking an extremely important series of experiments."

"For which you need a considerable amount of human material."

"A very considerable amount—which explains those drives we carry out in the jungle to renew our supplies. Unfortunately, it's the gorillas who organize them, and we can't stop them indulging in their favorite pastime, which is shooting. A large number of subjects have thus been lost to science."

"What a terrible shame," I muttered, biting my lip. "But to get back to me . . ."

"Do you know why I've insisted on keeping our secret?"

"Am I then condemned to spend the rest of my life in a cage?"

"Not if the plan I have in mind succeeds. But you must not drop your mask until the time is ripe and you hold all the cards. This is what I suggest: in a month from now we're holding our animal biological conference. It's an important event. A large public is admitted to it and the representatives of all the leading papers attend. Now, for us public opinion is a more powerful element than Zaius, more powerful than all the orangutans combined, more powerful even than the gorillas. This will be your chance. It's when this congress is in full session that you must lift the veil; for you're going to be introduced by Zaius, who, as I've told you, is preparing a long report on you and your famous instinct. The best thing then would be for you to speak up yourself to explain your case. This would cause such a sensation that Zaius wouldn't be able to stop you. It will be up to you to explain yourself clearly to the assembly and convince the crowd and the journalists, as you have already convinced me."

"And if Zaius and the orangutans put their foot down?"

"Once the gorillas are forced to bow before public opinion, they'll soon make those idiot orangutans see reason. Many of them, after all, are not so stupid as Zaius; and there are also, among the scientists, a few chimpanzees whom the Academy has been obliged to admit because of their sensational discoveries. One of these is Cornelius, my fiancé. He's the only one to whom I have spoken about you. He has promised to do all he can for you. Naturally, he wants to see you beforehand so as to check the incredible account I have given him. That's partly why I've brought you here today. I've arranged to meet him and he shouldn't be long."

Cornelius was waiting for us near a bank of giant ferns. He was a fine-looking chimpanzee, older than Zira certainly, but extremely young for a learned academician. As soon as I saw him I was struck by his exceptionally keen and intense expression.

"What do you think of him?" Zira whispered to me in French.

I realized from her question that I had definitely won the confidence of this she-ape. I muttered some complimentary remark and we went up to him.

The engaged couple embraced in the manner of the lovers in the park. He had opened his arms wide without glancing in my direction. In spite of what she had told him about me, it was clear that my presence counted no more for him than that of a pet animal. Zira herself forgot me for a moment and they exchanged long kisses on the muzzle. Then she stiffened, broke free from him, and bashfully lowered her eyes.

"Darling, we are not alone."

"Yes, I am here," I said with dignity in my best simian language.

"What's that?" Cornelius exclaimed with a start.

"I said, I am here. I am sorry to have to remind you of the fact. Your demonstrations do not embarrass me in the least, but you might hold it against me later."

"Well, I never!" exclaimed the learned chimpanzee. Zira burst out laughing and introduced us.

"Dr. Cornelius of the Academy," she said. "Ulysse Mérou, an inhabitant of the solar system or, to be more precise, the Earth."

"I am delighted to make your acquaintance," I said. "Zira has told me about you. I congratulate you on having such a charming fiancée."

And I held out my hand. He shied away as

though a snake had just raised its head in front of him.

"So, it's true?" he muttered, looking at Zira in utter bewilderment.

"Darling, am I in the habit of telling you lies?"

He pulled himself together. He was a man of science. After a moment's hesitation he shook my hand.

"How do you do?"

"How do you do?" I replied. "Once more I must apologize for appearing in this state of undress."

"That's all he can think of," said Zira with a laugh. "It's a complex with him. He does not realize the effect he would have if he were dressed."

"And you really come from . . . from . . . ?"

"From Earth, a planet of the Sun."

He had evidently given little credit till now to Zira's confidences, preferring to believe in some hoax. He started firing questions at me. We were strolling along, the two of them a few paces ahead and arm in arm, I following on the end of my chain so as not to attract the attention of the passers-by we chanced to meet. But my replies roused his scientific curiosity to such a pitch that he would often stop short, let go of his fiancée, and we would embark on a discussion face to face with sweeping gestures, tracing diagrams in the sand on the path. Zira did not mind. She appeared, on the contrary, delighted with the impression I had made.

Cornelius was particularly interested, of course, in the emergence of *Homo sapiens* on Earth and made me tell him again and again everything I knew about this subject. Then he pondered over it for some time. He told me that my revelations undoubtedly constituted a document of capital importance to science and particularly to him, as he was then engaged on some extremely arduous research into the simian phenomenon. From what I understood, this was still an unsolved problem to him and he did not agree with the generally accepted theories. But he became reticent on this subject and did not let me know his views completely during this first encounter.

However it might be, I was an object of great interest to him and he would have given a fortune to have me in his laboratory. We then spoke about my present situation and about Zaius, whose stupidity and blindness he fully appreciated. He approved of Zira's plan. He would himself prepare the ground by alluding to the mystery of my case in the presence of some of his colleagues.

When he left us he held out his hand without a moment's hesitation, after first making sure the path was deserted. Then he kissed his fiancée and went off, not without turning around several times to convince himself that I was not an hallucination.

"A charming young ape," I said as we made our way back to the car.

"And a very great scientist. With his support I'm sure you will persuade the congress."

"Zira," I murmured in her ear when I was in the back seat, "I shall owe you my liberty and my life."

I was thinking of all she had done for me since my capture. Without her I should never have been able to come into contact with the simian world. Zaius would have been quite capable of having my brain removed to demonstrate that I was not a rational being. Thanks to her, I now had some allies and could face the future with a little more optimism.

"I did it out of love for science," she said, blushing. "You are a unique case that must be preserved at all costs."

My heart overflowed with gratitude. I yielded to the soulfulness of her expression, managing to overlook her physical appearance. I put my hand on her long hairy paw. A shiver went down her spine and I discerned in her eyes a gleam of affection. We were both deeply moved and remained silent all the way back. When she returned me to my cage, I roughly rebuffed Nova, who was indulging in some sort of childish demonstration to welcome me back.

twenty-two

Zira has secretly lent me a flashlight and has slipped me some books that I keep hidden under the straw. I now read and speak the apes' language fluently. I spend several hours every night studying their civilization. Nova protested at first. She came over and sniffed at one of the books, baring her teeth as though it were a dangerous adversary. I only had to focus the beam of my flash on her to see her dash back into her corner, trembling and whimpering. I am the absolute master at home, now that I possess this instrument, and no longer need any arguments more striking to keep her quiet. I feel she looks upon me as a redoubtable being, and I notice from many signs that the other captives also regard me as such. My prestige has increased considerably, and I take unfair advantage of this. Sometimes I have an un-reasoning desire to terrify Nova by brandishing the flashlight, after which she creeps back to pardon me for my cruelty.

I flatter myself that I now have a fairly clear idea of the simian world.

The apes are not divided into nations. The whole planet is administered by a council of ministers, at the head of which is a triumvirate consisting of one gorilla, one orangutan, and one chimpanzee. In con-junction with this government, there is also a parlia-ment composed of three chambers: the Chamber of Gorillas, of Orangutans, and of Chimpanzees, each of which attends to the interests of its respective members.

In fact, this division into three races is the only one that exists. In principle they all have equal rights and are allowed to occupy any position. Yet, with certain exceptions, each species confines itself to its own specialty.

From far back in the past, when they used to reign by force, the gorillas have preserved a taste for authority and still form the most powerful class. They do not mingle with the herd, they are never seen at popular demonstrations, but it is they who administer at very high level most of the great enter-prises. Rather ignorant as a rule, they know by in-stinct how to make use of their skills. They excel in the art of drawing up general directives and han-dling the other apes. When a technician makes an interesting discovery—a luminous tube, for instance, or some new combustible fuel—it is almost always a gorilla who undertakes to exploit it and derive every possible benefit from it. Without being really intelligent, they are much more cunning than the orangutans. They get whatever they want out of the latter by playing on their pride. Thus, at the head of our institute, above Zaius who is the scientific director, there is a gorilla administrator who is rarely seen. He has come into our room only once. He looked me up and down with his particular air of authority, and I almost automatically rose to my feet and stood to attention. I noticed Zaius' servile attitude, and Zira herself seemed impressed by his grand manner.

The gorillas who do not occupy positions of authority are usually engaged on lesser jobs requiring physical strength. Zoram and Zanam, for instance, are there only for the rough work and especially for maintaining law and order when necessary.

Or else the gorillas are hunters. This is a function more or less reserved for them. They capture wild animals and, in particular, men. I have already pointed out the enormous numbers of men required for the apes' experiments. These experiments play a part in their lives that I find more disconcerting as I discover their importance. A large section of the simian population seems to be engaged in biological study, but I shall come back to this oddity later. However it may be, the supplying of human material necessitates an organized enterprise. A whole tribe of hunters, beaters, porters, and tradesmen is devoted to this industry, at the head of which there are always gorillas. I believe this is a prosperous business, for man fetches a high price.

By the side of the gorillas—I was going to say below them, although any form of hierarchy is contested—are the orangutans and the chimpanzees. The former, who are by far the least numerous, were described to me by Zira in a single phrase: they are official science.

This is partly true, but some of them occasionally indulge in politics, the arts, and literature. They bring the same characteristics to all these activities. Pompous, solemn, pedantic, devoid of originality and critical sense, intent on preserving tradition, blind and deaf to all innovation, they form the substratum of every academy. Endowed with a good memory, they learn an enormous amount by heart and from books. Then they themselves write other books, in which they repeat what they have read, thereby earning the respect of their fellow orangutans. Perhaps I am slightly biased in my attitude toward them by the opinion of Zira and her fiancé, who detest them, as do all the chimpanzees. Moreover, they are equally despised by the gorillas, who laugh at their lack of initiative but who exploit them for the benefit of their own schemes. Almost every orangutan has behind him a gorilla or a council of gorillas who support him and maintain him in an honorable post, seeing to it that he is granted the titles and decorations that are dear to his heart—until the day he ceases to give satisfaction. Then he is dismissed without mercy and replaced by another ape of the same species.

There remain the chimpanzees. These seem to represent the intellectual element of the planet. It is not an idle boast that all the great discoveries have been made by them, as Zira first told me. This is a slightly exaggerated generalization, for there are a few exceptions. In any case, they write most of the interesting books and on a great variety of subjects. They seem animated by a powerful spirit of research.

I have mentioned the sort of works the orangutans produce. The unfortunate thing is, as Zira frequently deplores, they thus write all the educational books, propagating grotesque errors among simian youth. Not long ago, she assures me, these school textbooks still stated that the planet Soror was the center of the world, although this heresy had been rejected long before by every ape of even mediocre intelligence; and the only reason for this was that there once existed on Soror, thousands of years ago, an ape of considerable authority called Haristas who held such beliefs and whose dogmas have been repeated by the orangutans ever since. It is easier to understand Zira's attitude toward me now that I have learned that this Haristas believed that apes alone can have a soul. The chimpanzees, fortunately, have a far more critical mind. In the last few years, it seems, they have embarked on a regular campaign to disparage the old idol's axioms.

As for the gorillas, they write very few books, and these are noteworthy more because of their appearance than their subject matter. I have glanced through some of them, and remember their titles: *The Need for Sound Organization as the Basis of Research, The Benefits of Social Politics,* or *The Organization of the Large Man Hunts on the Green Continent.* These works are always well documented, each chapter being written by a specialized technician, and contain diagrams, tables, and sometimes attractive photographs.

The unification of the planet, the absence of war and military expenditures—there is no army, only a police force—strike me as being factors that would foster rapid progress in every realm of the simian world. This is not the case. Although Soror is probably slightly older than the Earth, it is clear that the apes lag behind us in any number of ways.

They have electricity, industries, motor cars, and airplanes, but, as far as the conquest of space is concerned, they have reached only the stage of artificial satellites. In pure science I think their knowledge of the infinitely great and the infinitely small is inferior to ours. This backwardness is perhaps due to mere chance, and I have no doubt they will catch up with us one day, when I consider their capacity for application and the spirit of research shown by the chimpanzees. In fact, it seems to me they have been through a dark period of stagnation that has lasted a very long time, far longer than with us, and have only recently entered an age of considerable achievement.

This spirit of research, I must once again point out, is directed principally in one direction: the biological sciences and in particular the study of ape, man being the instrument they use to this end. The latter thus plays an essential, albeit rather humiliating, part in their existence. It is lucky that there is a considerable supply of men on their planet. I have read a paper proving there are more men here than apes. But the number of the latter is on the increase, whereas the human population is falling off, and already some scientists are anxious about future supplies for their laboratories.

All this does not explain the secret of simian evolution. On the other hand, perhaps there is no mystery about it. Their emergence is no doubt as natural as our own. Yet I cannot entirely accept this idea, and I now know that some of their scientists also consider that the phenomenon of simian ascendency is by no means clear. Cornelius belongs to this school, and I believe he is seconded by the keenest brains. Unaware of where they come from, who they are, or where they are going, they no doubt suffer from this lack of knowledge. Might it not be this feeling that inspires them with a sort of frenzy for biological research and that gives such a special slant to their scientific pursuits? My night-time meditation concludes with these questions.

twenty-three

Zira took me for outings in the park fairly often. Sometimes we would meet Cornelius there, and together we would prepare the speech I was to give before the congress. The date was fast approaching, which made me quite nervous. Zira assured me that all would be well. Cornelius was eager for my state to be recognized and my liberty restored so that he could study me closely—collaborate with me, he corrected himself, at the gesture of annoyance that escaped me when he spoke like this.

One day her fiancé was absent. Zira suggested going to the zoo adjoining the park. I should have liked to go to a theater or a museum, but these entertainments were still forbidden me. Only from books had I been able to acquire a few ideas about

simian art. I had admired some reproductions of
classical paintings, portraits of celebrated apes,
country scenes with lascivious she-apes around whom
fluttered a little winged monkey representing Cupid,
military paintings dating from the time when there
were still wars and depicting terrifying gorillas
wearing flamboyant uniforms. The apes had also
had their impressionists, and a few contemporaries
indulged in abstract art. All this I had discovered in
my cage, by the light of my flashlight. I could de-
cently attend only open-air entertainments. Zira
had taken me to see a game resembling our football,
a boxing match, which had made me shudder, between two gorillas, and an athletic meet in which
air-borne chimps launched themselves to prodigious heights by means of a springboard.

I welcomed a visit to the zoo. At first I felt no surprise. The animals bore many similarities to those
on Earth. There were felines, pachyderms, rumi-
nants, reptiles, and birds. If I noticed a sort of camel
with three humps and a wild boar with horns like a
stag, they could in no way astonish me after what I
had already seen on the planet Soror.

My amazement began with the section devoted
to man. Zira tried to dissuade me from going there,
regretting having brought me, I believe, but my curiosity was too strong and I tugged on my lead until
she yielded.

The first cage at which we stopped contained at
least fifty individuals, men, women, and children,

exhibited there to the great glee of the ape specta-
tors. They displayed a feverish and immoderate activity, leaping about, jostling one another, making
an exhibition of themselves, indulging in all sorts of
frolics.

It was certainly a sight. They were all intent on
winning favor with the little apes surrounding their
cage, who now and then threw them some fruit or
pieces of cake sold by an old she-ape at the entrance. It was the man, either adult or child, who
did the best trick—climbing up the bars, walking
on all fours or on his hands—who obtained the reward, and when this fell in the middle of a group,
there was a scuffle involving scratched faces and
torn-out hair, the whole punctuated by the shrill
cries of animals in a temper.

There were some men who were more composed
and did not take part in this fracas. They sat apart,
near the bars, and when they saw an ape brat
plunge his fingers into a bag they would stretch out
an imploring hand. The ape, if he was very young,
would often draw back in fright, but his parents or
his friends would tease him until he decided, still
trembling, to pass the reward from hand to hand.

The appearance of a man outside the cage provoked some surprise, no less among the captives
than in the simian audience. The former interrupted
their play for a moment to examine me with suspi-
cion, but since I stood quite still, refusing with dignity the offerings that the youngsters tried to hand

me, apes and men alike lost interest in me and I was able to observe everything in peace. The silliness of these creatures sickened me, and I felt myself hot with shame when I once again noted how closely they resembled me physically.

The other cages provided the same degrading spectacle. I was about to let myself be led off by Zira, with a heavy heart, when suddenly, and with a great effort, I stifled a cry of surprise. There in front of me, among the herd, I saw none other than my traveling companion, the leader and mastermind of our expedition, the famous Professor Antelle. Like me, he had been captured and, no doubt less fortunate, had then been sold to the zoo.

My joy at knowing he was alive and seeing him again was such that tears came into my eyes; then I shuddered at the condition to which this learned man had been reduced. My emotion gradually changed to a painful numbness when I noticed that his behavior was identical to the other men's. I could not doubt the evidence of my own eyes, in spite of the improbability of this behavior. He was among the group of quiet ones who did not take part in the scuffles but stretched their hands through the bars with a begging grimace. I watched him while he was doing this, and there was nothing in his attitude to reveal his true nature. A little ape gave him some fruit. The scientist took it, sat down, crossed his legs, and began to devour it greedily, looking at his benefactor with an eager eye, as though he hoped for another gesture of generosity. I wept anew at this sight. In a low voice I told Zira the reason for my tears. I should have liked to go up and speak to him but she dissuaded me vigorously. I could do nothing for him at the moment, and, in the emotion of meeting again, we risked causing a scene that would prejudice our common interests and might well ruin my own plans.

"After the congress," she told me, "when you have been recognized and accepted as a rational being, we will see about him."

She was right and I regretfully let myself be dragged away. On the way back to the car I told her all about the professor and his reputation on Earth in the scientific world. She pondered over this for some time and promised to do her best to get him out of the zoo. I was therefore a little more cheerful on my return to the institute, but that evening I refused the food the gorillas brought me.

twenty-four

During the week preceding the congress Zaius paid me several visits, multiplying the ridiculous tests, while his secretary filled several notebooks with observations and conclusions concerning me. I hypocritically did my best not to appear more intelligent than he wished.

The long-awaited day finally arrived, but it was only on the third day of the congress that they came to fetch me, the first two having been devoted to theoretical debates. I was kept informed of the proceedings by Zira. Zaius had already read a long report about me, presenting me as a man with particularly sharp instincts but totally devoid of the capacity for thought. Cornelius asked him a few leading questions to discover how, in that case, he explained certain

aspects of my behavior. This revived old disputes, and
the last discussion had been a stormy one. The scientists were divided into two groups: those who refused
to acknowledge that an animal had a soul of any sort,
and those who saw only a difference of degree between the mentality of beasts and that of apes. No
one of course suspected the real truth, except Cornelius and Zira. Yet Zaius' report described such surprising characteristics that, even though this imbecile
was not aware of the fact, it made a deep impression
on certain impartial observers, if not on the decorated
scientists, and a rumor began to spread around the
town that an absolutely extraordinary man had been
discovered.

Zira whispered in my ear as she took me out of
the cage, "There'll be a vast crowd and the whole of
the press. They're all on tenterhooks and know
there's something unusual afoot. It's excellent for
you. Take courage!"

I badly needed her moral support. I felt terribly
nervous. I had rehearsed my speech all night. I knew
it by heart and it was bound to convince the most
limited minds; but I was haunted by the fear that I
might not be allowed to speak.

The gorillas led me off to a caged-in truck and I
found myself among several other human subjects,
likewise considered worthy of being introduced to
the learned assembly because of some peculiarity
or other. We arrived outside an enormous building
surmounted by a cupola. Our guards led us into a

room furnished with cages, adjoining the assembly hall. There we waited at the scientists' pleasure. Every now and then a majestic gorilla, clothed in a sort of black uniform, pushed open the door and shouted out a number. Then the guards would put one of the men on a lead and drag him off. My heart thundered at each appearance of the usher. Through the half-opened door I could hear the hubbub in the hall, an occasional exclamation, and also bursts of applause.

Since the subjects were driven away immediately after their introduction, I eventually found myself alone in the room with the guards, feverishly going over the main passages of my speech. They had kept me till the end, like a star performer. The black gorilla appeared for the last time and called out my number. I rose to my feet quickly, took from the hands of a flabbergasted ape the lead he was about to fasten to my collar, and adjusted it myself. Then, flanked by two bodyguards, I entered the assembly hall with a firm tread. As soon as I had crossed the threshold I halted, dazzled and abashed.

I had seen many a strange sight since my arrival on Soror. I thought I was so accustomed to the apes and their actions that I could no longer be astonished by them. Yet confronted with the singularity and proportions of the scene before my eyes, I was seized with giddiness and once again asked myself if I was not dreaming.

I was in a gigantic amphitheater (which put me strangely in mind of Dante's conical inferno) of which every row of seats both around and above me was swarming with apes. There were several thousands of them. Never before had I seen so many apes gathered together; their multitude transcended the wildest dreams of my poor terrestrial imagination; their numbers overwhelmed me.

I stumbled and tried to pull myself together by looking for some guiding light in this crowd. The guards pushed me toward the center of a circle, resembling a circus arena, where a platform had been erected. I slowly glanced all around me. The tiers of apes rose as high as the ceiling, to a height that seemed to me incredible. The seats nearest me were occupied by the members of the congress, all of them learned scientists dressed in striped trousers and dark frock coats, all of them wearing decorations, almost all of a venerable age, and almost all orangutans. I made out, however, among their group a small number of gorillas and chimpanzees. I looked for Cornelius among the latter, but could not see him.

Beyond the authorities and behind a balustrade were several rows reserved for the junior colleagues of the scientists. A gallery at this level was for the journalists and photographers. Finally, still higher up and behind another barrier, surged the crowd, a simian public which, from the loud murmurs that greeted my appearance, was evidently in a state of great excitement.

I also tried to see Zira, who was bound to be sitting among the assistants. I felt I needed the support of a glance from her. There again I was disappointed and could not discern a single familiar face among the hellish throng of apes surrounding me.

I switched my gaze to the pontiffs. Each of them was seated in an armchair draped in red, whereas the rest were entitled only to stools or benches. Their appearance reminded me forcefully of Zaius. Their heads sunk almost to the level of their shoulders, one immensely long arm half folded and placed in front of them on a blotter, they scribbled down an occasional note or perhaps a childish drawing. In contrast to the excitement prevailing on the higher benches, they looked utterly listless. I had the feeling that my entrance and the announcement about me that had been made over a loudspeaker were only just sufficient to revive their flagging attention. In fact, I distinctly remember seeing three of these orangutans give a start and suddenly shake their heads, as though roused from a deep sleep.

Yet they were now all wide awake. My introduction was no doubt the high spot of the meeting, and I felt I was the cynosure of thousands of pairs of simian eyes with a variety of expressions ranging from indifference to enthusiasm.

My guards made me mount the platform where an impressive-looking gorilla was sitting. Zira had told me that the congress was presided over not by a scientist, as had once been the case—in those days the apes of science, left to their own devices, used to lose themselves in endless discussions without ever coming to a conclusion—but by an organizer. To the left of this important figure was his secretary, a chimpanzee, who was making a verbatim report of the meeting. To her right was a seat occupied in turn by each of the scientists who was to read a paper or introduce a subject. Zaius had just taken this seat amidst some lukewarm applause. Thanks to a system of loudspeakers in conjunction with some powerful projectors, nothing happening on the platform was lost even at the uppermost levels of the hall.

The president gorilla rang his bell, obtained silence, and announced he was giving the illustrious Zaius leave to speak for the purpose of introducing the man about whom he had already addressed the assembly. The orangutan then rose to his feet and began on his discourse. During this time I was doing my best to assume as intelligent an attitude as possible. When he spoke about me I bowed, putting my hand to my breast, which at first gave rise to some laughter that was promptly stifled by the bell. I quickly realized I was not advancing my cause by indulging in these tricks, which might be interpreted as the mere result of good training. I stood still, waiting for the end of his speech.

He summarized the conclusions of his report and described the tricks he was going to make me perform, the equipment for his damnable tests having been set up on the platform. He ended by declaring that, like certain birds, I was also capable of repeating a few words, and he hoped to be able to make me do this in front of the assembly. Then he turned around to me, picked up the box with its multiple fastenings, and handed it to me. But instead of manipulating the locks, I embarked on another sort of exercise.

My hour had come. I raised my hand, then, tugging gently on the lead held by a guard, I approached the microphone and addressed the president.

"Illustrious President," I said in my best simian language, "it is with the greatest pleasure that I shall open this box; it is with the utmost willingness, too, that I shall perform all the tricks in the program. Before beginning this task, however, which is rather an easy one for me, I beg permission to make an announcement that, I swear, will astonish this learned assembly."

I had articulated very clearly and each of my words drove home. The result was what I had anticipated. All the apes remained glued to their seats, dumfounded, holding their breath. The journalists even forgot to take notes, and none of the photographers had the presence of mind to record this historic moment.

The president gaped at me. As for Zaius, he seemed to be in a towering rage.

"Mr. President," he yelled, "I protest . . ."

But he stopped short, overwhelmed by the ridiculousness of a discussion with a man. I took advantage of this to go on with my speech.

"Mr. President, I insist with the greatest respect, but also with the utmost firmness, that this favor be granted me. Once I have explained myself, I swear on my honor that I shall bow to the demands of the very illustrious Zaius."

After a moment's silence, a hurricane shook the assembly. A raging storm swept the rows of seats, transforming all the apes into a hysterical mass in which were mingled exclamations, bursts of laughter, sobs, and cheers, all this in the midst of a continuous flash of magnesium, the photographers having at last recovered the use of their limbs. The tumult lasted a good five minutes, during which the president, who had recovered some of his composure, never took his eyes off me. He eventually came to a decision and rang his bell.

"I . . ." he stammered, "I really don't know how to address you."

"Just call me *monsieur*," I said.

"Yes, well, er . . . *monsieur,* I think that, in view of the exceptional nature of the case, the scientific congress over which I have the honor to preside is entitled to listen to your announcement."

A fresh wave of applause greeted this decision. I did not ask for more. I stood bolt upright in the middle of the platform, adjusted the microphone to my height, and started the following speech.

twenty-five

"Illustrious President,
   "Noble Gorillas,
   "Learned Orangutans,
   "Wise Chimpanzees,
   "O Apes!
   "I, a man, beg leave to address you.

   "I know my appearance is grotesque, my figure repulsive, my features bestial, my smell sickening, the color of my skin disgusting. I know the sight of this ridiculous body of mine offends you, but I also know I am addressing the wisest and most learned apes of all, those whose minds are capable of rising above mere sensory impressions and of perceiving the essential substance of a being apart from his wretched material exterior. . . ."

The pompous humility of this opening had been suggested by Zira and Cornelius, who knew it was liable to touch the orangutans. I went on in a silence that was complete:

"Listen to me, O Apes! For I can talk, and not, I assure you, like a mechanical toy or a parrot. I can think, I can talk, I can understand what you say just as well as what I myself say. Presently, if Your Lordships deign to question me, I shall deem it an honor to reply to your questions to the best of my ability.

"But first I should like to reveal this astounding truth to you: not only am I a rational creature, not only does a mind paradoxically inhabit this human body, but I come from a distant planet, from Earth, that Earth on which, by a whim of nature that has still to be explained, it is men who are the repositories of wisdom and reason. I beg permission to point out the place of my origin, not of course for the benefit of the illustrious doctors whom I see all around me, but for those of my audience who perhaps are not so well acquainted with the various stellar systems."

I went up to a blackboard and by means of a few diagrams described the solar system to the best of my ability and indicated its position in the galaxy. My lecture was listened to in profound silence. But when, having finished my sketches, I clapped my hands together to get rid of the chalk dust on them, this simple gesture provoked an enthusiastic murmur among the crowd in the upper rows. I went, on facing my public:

"Thus on Earth the intellect is embodied in the human race. This is a fact and I can do nothing about it. Whereas the apes—and since discovering your world I am deeply upset about this—whereas the apes have remained in a state of savagery, it is the men who have evolved. It is in man's cranium that the brain has developed and flourished. It is man who invented language, discovered fire, made use of tools. It is man who settled my planet and changed its face, man, in fact, who established a civilization so refined that in many respects, O Apes, it resembles your own."

At this point I quoted several examples of our finest achievements. I described our cities, our industries, our means of communication, our governments, our laws, our entertainments. Then I addressed myself more specifically to the learned authorities and tried to give them an idea of our conquest in the noble fields of the sciences and arts. My voice became firmer the longer I spoke. I began to feel a sort of intoxication, like an owner taking stock of his possessions.

I then embarked on the account of my own adventures. I described the means by which I had reached the world of Betelgeuse and landed on the planet Soror, how I had been captured and locked up in a cage, how I tried to enter into contact with Zaius, and how, doubtless as a result of my lack of ingenuity, all my efforts had been in vain. Lastly I mentioned Zira's perspicacity, her valuable assistance and that of Dr. Cornelius. I concluded with the following words:

"This is what I wanted to tell you, O Apes! It is up to you now to decide whether I should be treated like an animal and end my days in a cage after such astonishing adventures. It remains for me to say that I voyaged here without any hostile intent, inspired solely by the spirit of discovery. Since I have come to know you I find you extraordinarily congenial and I admire you with all my heart. This, then, is the plan I suggest to the great minds of this planet. I can certainly be useful to you by virtue of my earthly knowledge; for my part, I have learned more things during a few months' captivity among you than in all my previous existence. Let us unite our efforts! Let us establish contacts with the Earth! Let us march forward hand in hand, apes and men together, and no power, no secret of the cosmos will be able to resist us!"

I stopped speaking, exhausted, in total silence. I turned automatically to the president's table, picked up the glass of water standing there, and drained it in a gulp. Like the act of clapping my hands together, this simple gesture produced an amazing effect and was the signal for an absolute uproar. The whole hall spontaneously gave vent to an enthusiastic outburst that no pen could ever describe. I knew I had won over my audience, but I would never have thought it possible for any assembly in the world to break into such commotion. I was deafened by it, retaining just enough composure to observe one of the reasons for this fantastic din: apes, who are exuberant by nature, clap with all four hands when they are pleased. I was thus surrounded by a seething mass of frantic creatures balancing on their rumps and waving their four limbs in a frenzy of applause punctuated by wild yells in which the gorillas' deep voices predominated. This was one of my last glimpses of this memorable session. I felt unsteady on my feet. I looked anxiously around me. Zaius had just risen from his seat in fury and was striding up and down the platform with his hands behind his back, as he did in front of my cage. As though in a dream, I saw the vacant chair and collapsed into it. A fresh burst of applause, which I barely heard before fainting dead away, greeted this gesture.

twenty-six

It was some time before I recovered consciousness, so intense had been the strain of this session. I found myself lying on a bed in a room. Zira and Cornelius were attending me, while some gorillas in uniform held back a crowd of journalists and curious onlookers who were trying to approach me.

"Magnificent!" Zira whispered in my ear. "You've won."

"Ulysse," said Cornelius, "together we're going to do great things."

He told me that the Grand Council of Soror had just held a special meeting and had decided on my immediate release.

"There were some who opposed it," he added,

"but public opinion demanded it and they had to yield."

Having himself requested and obtained permission to take me on as his collaborator, he was rubbing his hands at the thought of the assistance I would provide in his research.

"This is where you'll be living. I hope this apartment will suit you. It is quite close to mine, in a wing of the institute reserved for the senior personnel."

I looked around in bewilderment, thinking I was dreaming. The room was provided with every comfort; it was the beginning of a new epoch. After hoping so long for this moment, I was suddenly overwhelmed by an odd feeling of nostalgia. My eyes met Zira's and I saw that the clever she-ape had read my thoughts. A rather ambiguous smile came over her face.

"Here, of course," she said, "you won't have Nova with you."

I blushed, shrugged my shoulders, and sat up. I had recovered my strength and was eager to embark on my new life.

"Do you feel well enough to attend a little party?" Zira asked. "We've invited a few friends, all of them chimpanzees, to celebrate this great day."

I replied that nothing would give me greater pleasure, but I was no longer willing to appear stark naked. I then noticed I was wearing some pajamas, Cornelius having lent me his. But though I was able, in a pinch, to wear a chimpanzee's pajamas, I should have looked grotesque in one of his suits.

"We'll fit you out completely tomorrow and you'll have a decent suit for this evening. Here's the tailor."

A little chimpanzee came in and greeted me with great courtesy. I discovered that while I was still lying unconscious, the best tailors had competed for the honor of dressing me. This one, the most famous of all, had the most noted gorillas in the capital as clients.

I admired his speed and dexterity. In less than two hours he had succeeded in making me an acceptable suit. It felt quite strange to be wearing clothes again, and Zira looked at me as though she had never seen me before. While the artist was making the final adjustments Cornelius admitted the journalists who were hammering at the door. I was put through a catechism for over an hour, riddled with questions, under fire from the photographers, and required to furnish the most intriguing details about the Earth and the life men led on that planet. I lent myself willingly to this ceremony. A journalist myself, I realized the scoop I represented to these colleagues and knew what a powerful support the press could be.

It was late by the time they left. We were just on our way to join Cornelius' friends when we were detained by the arrival of Zanam. He was obviously acquainted with the latest developments, for he gave me an obsequious bow. He had come to tell Zira that things were not going too well in her department. Furious at my long absence, Nova was making a great racket. Her mood had infected all the other captives, and no amount of pike blows would calm them down.

"I'll go and see," said Zira. "Wait for me here."

I looked at her with a pleading expression. She hesitated, then shrugged her shoulders.

"Come along if you like," she said. "After all, you're free and perhaps you'll be able to calm them down better than I can."

Together we entered the room with the cages. The captives calmed down as soon as they saw me, and the uproar was followed by a strange silence. They recognized me in spite of my clothes and seemed to understand that they were in the presence of something miraculous.

Trembling with emotion, I walked over to Nova's cage, my own cage. I went right up to her, I smiled at her, I spoke to her. For a moment I had the impression that she was following my train of thought and was about to answer me. This was impossible, but my mere presence had calmed her down like the others. She accepted a lump of sugar that I handed to her and ate it while I made my way out of the room with a heavy heart.

Of that party, which took place in a smart night club—Cornelius had decided to launch me forthwith into simian society, since in any case I was now destined to live in it—I have only a confused and rather disturbing memory.

The confusion was caused by the alcohol that I started swilling as soon as I arrived, and to which my system was no longer accustomed. The disturbing effect was an odd sensation that was to come over me later on many other occasions. I can only describe it by saying that the nature of the figures around me became progressively less simian, whereas their function or the position they held in society became dominant. The head waiter, for instance, who came up obsequiously to show us our table, I saw only as the *head waiter*, and the fact that he was a gorilla tended to be obscured. The figure of an elderly she-ape with an outrageously painted face was replaced by that of an *old coquette*, and when I danced with Zira I forgot her condition completely, and my arm merely encircled the waist of a dancer. The chimpanzee orchestra was nothing more than an orchestra, and the elegant apes exchanging witticisms all around me were simply men about town.

I shall not dwell on the sensation caused by my presence among them. I was the focus of all eyes. I had to give my autograph to a number of fans, and the two gorillas whom Cornelius had had the prudence to bring along were hard-pressed to protect me from the swarm of she-apes of every age who competed for the honor of having a drink or dancing with me.

It was getting late and I was already fairly tipsy when the thought of Professor Antelle crossed my mind. I felt steeped in black remorse. I was not far from shedding a tear or two over my own infamy as I reflected that here I was making merry and drinking with a lot of apes while my companion was shivering on some straw in a cage.

Zira asked me why I was looking so sad. I told her. Cornelius then informed me that he had made inquiries about the professor and that he was in good health. There would be no opposition now to his being released. I insisted that I could not wait a minute longer before bringing him this good news.

"After all," Cornelius agreed, after thinking it over, "one can't refuse you anything on a day like this. Let's go. I know the director of the zoo."

The three of us left the night club and drove to the garden. On being waked up, the director bestirred himself. He knew all about me. Cornelius told him the true identity of one of the men he held locked up in a cage. He could hardly believe his ears, but he, too, was eager to do all he could for me. We should have to wait, of course, until the next day and go through various formalities before he could release the professor, but meanwhile there was nothing against our having a talk with him at once. He offered to accompany us.

Day was breaking when we reached the cage in which the luckless scientist lived like an animal in the midst of fifty men and women. These were still asleep, huddled together in couples or in groups of four or five. They opened their eyes as soon as the director switched on the lights.

It did not take me long to find my companion. He was stretched out on the ground like the others, huddled against the body of a girl who looked quite young. I shuddered to see him like this, and at the same time was moved by the debasement to which I, too, had been reduced for four months.

I was so upset that I could not speak. The men, who were now awake, showed no sign of surprise. They were tame and well trained; they began performing their usual tricks in the hope of some reward. The director threw them some pieces of cake. Immediately scuffles and disputes broke out, as they did during the day, while the quietest of them assumed their favorite position, squatting by the bars and stretching out an imploring hand.

Professor Antelle followed their example. He came up as close as possible to the director and begged for a titbit. This humiliating behavior gave me a sickening feeling that soon became an unbearable anguish. He was three paces away; he was looking at me and appeared not to recognize me. In fact, his eyes, which had once been so keen, had lost all their gleam and suggested the same spiritual void as those of the other captives. I was horrified to see in them no more emotion than that aroused among the other captives by the presence of a man in clothes.

I made a great effort and managed at last to speak in order to put an end to this nightmare.

"Professor," I said, "Master, it is I, Ulysse Mérou. We are saved. I came here to tell you . . ."

I stopped in sheer amazement. At the sound of my voice he had reacted in the same way as the men of the planet Soror. He had suddenly lowered his head and shrunk away.

"Professor, Professor Antelle," I beseeched him, "it's I, Ulysse Mérou, your traveling companion. I am free, and in a few hours you will be too. These apes you see here are our friends. They know who we are and welcome us like brothers."

There was no response. He showed not the slightest sign of comprehension but, with another frightened gesture like that of a startled beast, recoiled still further.

I was in despair, and the apes seemed extremely puzzled. Cornelius wrinkled his brow, as he did when he was trying to find the solution to a problem. It crossed my mind that the professor, frightened by their presence, might well be pretending to be witless. I asked them to move away and leave me alone with him, to which they readily agreed. When they had disappeared, I walked around the cage to reach the corner in which the scientist had taken refuge and again I spoke to him:

"Master," I implored him, "I understand your caution. I know the danger to which men from Earth are exposed on this planet. But we are alone, I give you my word of honor, and our ordeals are over. You must believe me, your companion, your disciple, your friend, Ulysse Mérou."

He shrank back still further, darting furtive glances in my direction. Then, while I stood there trembling, not knowing what else to say, he half opened his mouth.

Had I succeeded at last in convincing him? I watched him, hoping against hope. But I remained speechless with horror at the manner in which he expressed his emotion. I said that he had half opened his mouth, but this was not the spontaneous gesture of a creature preparing to speak. He emitted from it a gurgling sound similar to those uttered by the strange men on this planet to express satisfaction or fear. There in front of me, without moving his lips, while my heart went numb with horror, Professor Antelle gave vent to a long-drawn-out howl.

THREE

twenty-seven

I woke early after a restless night. I turned over three or four times in my bed and rubbed my eyes before fully recovering consciousness, still unaccustomed to the civilized life I had been leading for a month, feeling anxious every morning at not hearing the straw creak and not feeling Nova's warmth against me.

I eventually came to my senses. I was living in one of the most comfortable apartments in the institute. The apes had proved extremely generous. I had a bedroom, a bathroom, clothes, books, a television set. I read all the papers, I was free, I could go out, walk about the streets, attend any entertainment. My presence in a public place still provoked considerable interest, but the emotion of the first few days had started to die down.

Cornelius was now the scientific head of the institute. Zaius had been dismissed—he had been given another post, however, and a new decoration—and Zira's fiancé installed in his place. This had resulted in a reorganization of the personnel, a general promotion of the chimpanzee element, and renewed activity in every department. Zira had become the new director's assistant.

As for me, I took part in the scientist's research work, no longer as a guinea pig but as a collaborator. However, it was only with great difficulty and after much hesitation on the part of the Grand Council that Cornelius had been granted this favor. The authorities still appeared reluctant to admit my nature and origin.

I dressed quickly, left my room, and walked over to the wing of the institute where I had once been a prisoner: the department under Zira, who was still directing it in addition to her new duties. With Cornelius' permission I had embarked there on a systematic study of the men.

Here I am in the room with the cages, walking along the corridor in front of the bars like one of the masters of this planet. Shall I admit that I come here frequently, more frequently than my duties demand? There are times when I feel burdened by constantly simian surroundings, and here I find a sort of refuge.

The captives are well acquainted with me now and recognize my authority. Do they see any difference between me, Zira, and the warders who bring them their food? I should like to think so, but I doubt it. For the last month, despite my patience and efforts, I, too, have been unsuccessful in making them achieve any higher level of performance than that of well-trained animals. A secret intuition tells me, however, that their potentialities are enormous.

I should like to teach them to talk. This is my great ambition. I have not succeeded, I admit. It is only with the utmost difficulty that some of them manage to repeat a monosyllabic sound or two, which certain chimpanzees on Earth can do. It is not much, but I am persevering. What encourages me is the new persistence with which their eyes try to meet mine, eyes which for some time have seemed to be gradually changing in expression. I fancy I can see in them a spark of curiosity, associated with a superior mentality, breaking through the animal mindlessness.

I move slowly around the room, stopping in front of each of the captives. I speak to them; I speak to them gently, patiently. They are now accustomed to this unusual behavior on my part. They seem to listen. I go on for several minutes, then stop speaking in whole sentences and pronounce a few simple words, repeating them over and over again, hoping for an echo. One of them clumsily articulates a syllable, but this is as far as he will go today. The subject soon gets tired, abandons the superhuman task, and lies down on the floor as though after some exhausting effort. I sigh and pass on to the next one. I finally come to the cage in which Nova is at present vegetating in solitary sadness. Sadness— this at least is what I, with my Earthman's conceit, wish to believe, and I struggle to detect this emotion on her beautiful but inexpressive features. Zira has not given her another mate, and I am grateful for that.

I often think of Nova. I cannot forget the hours I spent in her company. But I have never again entered her cage; human self-respect forbids me. Is she not an animal? I now live in the highest scientific circles; how could I let myself indulge in such a relationship? I blush at the thought of our former intimacy. Since I have changed camps I have even forbidden myself to show her more affection than I show to her fellows.

Nevertheless I cannot help noting that she is an exceptional subject and I am glad of that. With her I obtain better results than with the others. She presses up against the bars as soon as she sees me, and her mouth twists into a grimace that could almost pass as a smile. Even before I have opened my mouth she tries to pronounce the three of four syllables she has learned. Her diligence is evident. Is she naturally more gifted than the others? Or has contact with me polished her and given her a capacity to benefit more from my lessons? I like to think, with a certain complacency, that this is the case.

I say her name, then my own, pointing my finger alternately at her and myself. She imitates the gesture. But I see her expression change suddenly and she bares her teeth as I hear a gentle chuckle behind me.

It is Zira, who laughs not unkindly at my efforts; her presence always rouses the girl to anger. Zira is accompanied by Cornelius, who is interested in my efforts and often comes to see the results for himself. Today he has come to see me for another reason. He looks rather excited.

"Would you like to go on a little trip with me, Ulysse?"

"A trip?"

"Quite a long one; almost to the antipodes. Some archeologists have discovered some extremely curious ruins out there, if the reports reaching us are to be believed. An orangutan is directing the excavations and he can scarcely be relied upon to interpret the vestiges correctly. There's something strange about them that fascinates me and that may afford decisive material for my research. The Academy is sending me out there on an official mission and I think your presence would be most useful."

I do not see how I can help him, but I welcome this opportunity to see further aspects of Soror. He takes me to his office to give me more details.

I am delighted by this diversion, which is an excuse for not completing my rounds; for there is one more prisoner for me to see—Professor Antelle. He is still in the same state, which makes his release impossible. Thanks to me, however, he is now on his own, isolated in a fairly comfortable cell. It is a painful duty for me to visit him. He replies to none of my earnest requests and still behaves like a perfect animal.

twenty-eight

We set off a week later. Zira came with us, but she was to return after a few days to look after the institute in Cornelius' absence. The latter intended staying much longer on the site of the excavations, if these proved to be as interesting as he expected.

A special plane had been put at our disposal, a jet machine rather like our first models of this type of aircraft, but very comfortable and equipped with a small soundproof compartment in which we could talk easily. It was here we were sitting, Zira and I, shortly after our departure. I was looking forward to the journey. By now I was completely accustomed to the simian world. I had been neither surprised nor frightened at seeing this big aircraft being piloted by an ape. My only thought was to enjoy the view and the spectacular sight of Betelgeuse rising. We had climbed to a height of about thirty thousand feet. The air was remarkably pure, and the giant star could be seen on the horizon like our own sun observed through a telescope. Zira was enchanted by it.

"Are there such beautiful dawns as this on Earth?" she asked. "Is your sun as lovely as ours?"

I told her it was neither as big nor as red, but it sufficed us. On the other hand, our nocturnal heavenly body was bigger and shed a more intense pale light than Soror's. We felt as happy as school children on a holiday, and I laughed and joked with her as with a very close friend. When Cornelius came and joined us after a moment I almost resented his intrusion on our tête à tête. He was pensive. For some time, moreover, he had seemed rather nervous. He worked prodigiously on his own research, which absorbed him to the point of occasionally causing him to be totally absent-minded. He still kept the subject of this research a secret, and I believe Zira knew as little about it as I did. I only knew it concerned the origin of ape and that the learned chimpanzee tended more and more to reject the classical theories. This morning, for the first time, he revealed certain aspects of it to me, and it did not take me long to understand why my existence as a civilized man was so important to him. He began by reverting to a subject we had discussed together a thousand times.

"You did say, didn't you, Ulysse, that on your Earth the apes are utter animals? That man has risen to a degree of civilization equal to our own and which, in certain respects, even . . . ? Don't be frightened of making me angry; the scientific spirit ignores all self-esteem."

"Which, in many respects, even surpasses it—yes, that's undeniable. One of the best proofs is that I am here. It seems to me you have only reached the stage . . ."

"I know, I know," he broke in wearily. "We've discussed all that. We are now penetrating the secrets you discovered centuries ago. . . . And it's not only your statements that disturb me," he went on, nervously pacing up and down the little cabin. "For some time I've been harassed by a feeling—a feeling supported by certain concrete indications—that the key to these secrets, even here on our planet, has been held by other brains in the distant past."

I might have replied that this impression of rediscovery had also affected certain minds on Earth. Perhaps it even prevailed universally and possibly served as the basis for our belief in God. But I was careful not to interrupt him. He was following a train of thought that was still confused, which he expressed in an extremely reticent manner.

"Other brains," he repeated pensively, "that maybe were not . . ."

He broke off abruptly. He looked miserable, as

though tortured by the perception of a truth his mind was unwilling to admit.

"You did say, didn't you, that your apes possess a highly developed sense of mimicry?"

"They mimic us in everything we do, I mean in every act that does not demand a rational process of thought. So much so that with us the verb *ape* is synonymous with *imitate*."

"Zira," Cornelius murmured, as though depressed, "is it not this sense of *aping* that characterizes us as well?"

Without giving Zira time to protest, he went on excitedly, "It begins in childhood. All our education is based on imitation."

"It's the orangutans . . ."

"That's it. They are of tremendous importance, since it is they who mold our youth through their books. They force every young monkey to repeat all the errors of his ancestors. That explains the slowness of our progress. For the last two thousand years we have remained similar to ourselves."

This slow development among the apes deserves a few comments. I had been struck by it while reading their history, noticing in it some important differences from the soaring flight of the human mind. True, we also have known a period of semi-stagnation. We, too, have had our orangutans, our falsified education and ridiculous curricula, and this period lasted a long time.

Not so long, however, as in the apes' case, and

above all not at the same stage of evolution. The dark ages that the chimpanzee deplored had lasted about ten thousand years. During this period no notable progress had been achieved except, perhaps, during the last half century. But what I found extremely curious was that their earliest legends, their earliest chronicles, their earliest *memories* bore witness to a civilization that was already well advanced and in fact was more or less similar to that of the present day. These documents, ten thousand years old, afforded proof of general skills and achievements comparable to the skills and achievements of today; and, before them, there was a total blank: no tradition either oral or written, not a single clue. In essence, it seemed as though the simian civilization had made a miraculous appearance out of the blue ten thousand years before and had since been preserved more or less without modification. The ordinary ape had grown accustomed to finding this quite natural, never imagining a different state of mental development, but a perceptive brain like Cornelius' sensed an enigma there and was tormented by it.

"There are apes capable of original creation," Zira protested.

"Certainly," Cornelius agreed. "That's true, especially in recent years. In the long run, mind is able to embody itself in gesture. It has to, in fact; that's the natural course of evolution. . . . But what I'm passionately seeking Zira, what I'm trying to find out, is how it all began. . . . At present it strikes me as not impossible that it was through simple imitation at the beginning of our era."

"Imitation of what, of whom?"

He had reverted to his reticent manner and lowered his eyes as though regretting he had said too much.

"I can't answer that question yet," he finally said. "I need certain evidence. Perhaps we shall find it in the ruins of the buried city. According to the reports it existed much earlier than ten thousand years ago, in a period about which we know nothing."

twenty-nine

Cornelius has not told me anything more and I feel he is reluctant to do so, but what I already detect in his theories gives me a strange elation.

The archeologists have laid bare a whole city, buried in the sands of a desert, a city of which nothing remains, alas, but ruins. But these ruins, I am convinced, hold an extraordinary secret that I have vowed to solve. This should be possible for anyone who can observe and deduce, which the orangutan who is directing the excavations seems hardly capable of doing. He welcomed Cornelius with the respect due his senior position but with barely concealed contempt for his youth and the original ideas he sometimes expressed.

Digging among stones that crumble at every move

and in sand that sinks under every step is no easy job. It is now a month since we have been at it. Zira left us some time ago, but Cornelius insists on prolonging his stay. He is as enthusiastic as I am and convinced that only here, among these relics of the past, is to be found the solution to the great problems tormenting him.

The extent of his knowledge is really remarkable. First of all, he insisted on verifying personally the antiquity of the city. For this the apes have a process similar to our own, involving deep-rooted principles of chemistry, physics, and geology. On this point the chimpanzee is in agreement with the official scientists: the city is very, very old indeed. It is much more than ten thousand years old, and therefore constitutes a unique record, tending to show that simian civilization did not burst forth miraculously out of the void.

Something existed before this present era. But what? After this month of feverish investigation we are disappointed, for it seems that this prehistoric city was not very different from those of the present day. We have discovered remnants of houses, traces of factories, vestiges showing that these forebears had motor cars and airplanes, just as apes of today do. These remains indicate that the origins of mind can be traced far back into the past. This is less than Cornelius was expecting, I feel; it is less than I was hoping for.

This morning Cornelius has gone ahead of me to

the spot where the workmen have laid bare a house with thick walls made of a sort of reinforced concrete, which seems better preserved than the rest. The inside is filled with sand and debris that they have undertaken to sift. Until yesterday they had found nothing more than in the other sections: fragments of piping, household appliances, kitchen equipment. I am still idling outside the tent that I share with the scientist. From here I can see the orangutan giving his orders to the foreman, a chimpanzee with a crafty look in his eye. I cannot see Cornelius. He is in the trench with the workmen. He often takes a hand in the digging, for fear they might do something stupid and thereby lose an interesting item.

Here he is emerging from the hole, and it does not take me long to realize he has made an exceptional discovery. He is holding in his hand a small object that I cannot make out. He thrusts aside the old orangutan who tries to take it from him and puts it down on the ground with infinite care. He looks in my direction and beckons me over. As I approach I am struck by the change in his expression.

"Ulysse. Ulysse!"

Never have I seen him in such a state. He can barely talk. The workmen, who have also climbed out of the trench, gather around the find and prevent me from seeing it. They point it out to one another but they seem merely amused. Some of them laugh out loud. They are almost all hefty gorillas. Cornelius tells them to keep their distance.

"Ulysse!"

"Whatever is it?"

I see the object lying in the sand at the same moment that he mutters in a strangled voice:

"A doll, Ulysse, a doll!"

It is a doll, an ordinary china doll. By a miracle it has been preserved almost intact, with vestiges of hair and eyes that still reveal a few chips of color. It is such a familiar sight to me that at first I cannot understand Cornelius' emotion. It takes me several seconds to realize . . . then I've got it! It's strangeness dawns on me and immediately I am overwhelmed. It is a *human* doll representing a little girl, a little girl like one on Earth. But I refuse to let myself be taken in. Before proclaiming a miracle, every possibility of a more commonplace cause must be examined. A scientist like Cornelius must have done so already. Let us see: The dolls of child apes do include a few—a very few, but nevertheless a few—that have an animal or even human form. So it cannot be the mere presence of this one that moves my chimpanzee so deeply. . . . Let us go a step further: The toys of child apes representing animals are not made of china; and above all they are not usually *clothed*; in any case, not clothed like rational creatures. And this doll, I tell you, is clothed like a doll at home—the remnants of a frock, a blouse, a skirt and knickers can still be clearly seen—

dressed with the taste that a little girl on Earth might show in adorning her favorite doll, with the care that a little she-ape on Soror would take to clothe her ape doll, a care that she would never, *never* show to dress up an animal figure like the human figure. I realize, I realize more and more clearly, the reason for my clever chimpanzee's emotion.

And this is not all. The toy presents another anomaly, another oddity that makes all the workmen laugh and even provokes a smile from the solemn orang-utan directing the excavations. The doll *talks*. It talks like a doll at home. In putting it down, Cornelius happened to press the mechanism, which has been preserved intact, and it talked. Oh, it was not much of a speech! It uttered one word, one simple word of two syllables: *pa-pa*. "Papa," the doll repeats as Cornelius picks it up again and turns it round and round in his nimble hands. The word is the same in French and in the simian language, and no doubt in many other languages of this mysterious cosmos, and it has the same meaning. "Papa," the little human doll repeats, and this, above all, is what makes my learned companion's muzzle turn red; this is what affects me so deeply that I have to make an effort not to cry aloud as he leads me aside, bringing his precious discovery with him.

"The monstrous imbecile!" he mutters after a long silence.

I know whom he means and I share his indignation. The old orangutan with all his decorations has seen nothing more in it than a simple child ape's toy that an eccentric manufacturer living in the distant past has endowed with speech. It is useless to suggest another explanation to him. Cornelius does not even try to do so. The one that comes naturally to his mind, however, seems so disturbing that he keeps it to himself. He does not breathe a word of it even to me, but he knows that I have guessed it.

He remains wrapped in thought and silent for the rest of the day. I have the impression he is now frightened of pursuing his research and is regretting his semi-revelations. Now that his excitement has subsided, he is sorry I have witnessed his discovery.

On the very next day I am given proof that he regrets having brought me here with him. After a night's reflection he informs me, avoiding my eyes, that he has decided to send me back to the institute, where I shall be able to continue with more important work than in these ruins. My seat on the aircraft is booked. I shall be leaving in twenty-four hours.

thirty

Suppose, I argue, that men once reigned as masters on this planet. Suppose that a human civilization similar to ours flourished on Soror more than ten thousand years ago. . . .

This is no longer a senseless hypothesis—quite the contrary. No sooner do I formulate it than I feel the excitement produced by picking up the right scent among so many false ones. It is on this track, I know, that the solution to the irritating simian mystery is to be found. I realize my subconscious has always been dreaming of some explanation of this sort.

I am in the aircraft taking me back to the capital, accompanied by Cornelius' secretary, a rather talkative chimpanzee. I don't feel like chatting with him. I always tend to meditate when I'm in an airplane. I shall find no better opportunity than this voyage to put my thoughts in order.

Suppose, then, the existence in the distant past of a civilization on the planet Soror similar to our own. It is possible that creatures devoid of intelligence could have perpetuated it by a simple process of imitation? The answer to this question seems risky, but after thinking it over, a host of arguments occur to me that gradually lessen its aspect of unreasonableness. That perfected machines may one day succeed us is, I remember, an extremely commonplace notion on Earth. It prevails not only among poets and romantics but in all classes of society. Perhaps it is because it is so widespread, born spontaneously in popular imagination, that it irritates scientific minds. Perhaps it is also for this very reason that it contains a germ of truth. Only a germ: Machines will always be machines; the most perfected robot, always a robot. But what of living creatures possessing a certain degree of intelligence, like apes? And apes, *precisely,* are endowed with a keen sense of imitation. . . .

I close my eyes. I let myself be lulled by the drone of the engines. I feel the need to commune with myself in order to justify my position.

What is it that characterizes a civilization? Is it the exceptional genius? No, it is everyday life. . . . Hmm! Let us give intelligence its due. Let us concede that it is principally the arts, and first and foremost, literature. Is the latter really beyond the reach of our higher apes, if it is admitted that they are capable of stringing words together? Of what is our literature made? Masterpieces? Again, no. But once an original book has been written—and no more than one or two appear in a century—men of letters *imitate* it, in other words, they copy it so that hundreds of thousands of books are published on exactly the same theme, with slightly different titles and modified phraseology. This should be able to be achieved by apes, who are essentially imitators, provided, of course, that they are able to make use of language.

In fact, language represents the only valid objection. But wait a moment! It is not essential that apes should understand what they are copying in order to produce a hundred thousand volumes from a single original. It is clearly no more necessary for them than it is for us. Like us, they merely need to be able to repeat sentences after having heard them. All the rest of the literary process is purely mechanical. It is at this point that the opinion of certain learned biologists assumes its full value: There is nothing in the anatomy of the ape, they maintain, that precludes the use of speech—nothing, that is, except the necessary urge. It is not difficult to conceive that this urge came to him one day as a result of some sudden mutation.

The perpetuation of a literature like ours by talking apes does not, therefore, conflict with common sense in any way. Subsequently, perhaps, some *apes of letters* raised themselves a step or two higher on the intellectual ladder. As my learned friend Cornelius said, mind embodied itself in gesture—in this case, in the mechanism of speech—and a few original ideas were able to appear in the new simian world at the rate of one every century—as in our own case.

Cheerfully pursuing this train of thought, I soon succeeded in convincing myself that well-trained animals might well have been able to produce the paintings and sculptures I had admired in the museums of the capital and, in general, become expert in all the human arts, including the art of cinematography.

Having first considered the highest manifestations of intelligence, it was only too easy to extend my thesis to other areas. That of industry quickly succumbed to my analysis. It seemed absolutely clear that industry did not require the presence of a rational being to maintain itself. Basically, industry consisted of manual laborers, always performing the selfsame tasks, who could easily be replaced by apes; and, at a higher level, of executives whose function was to draft certain reports and pronounce certain words under given circumstances. All this was a question of conditioned reflexes. At the still higher level of administration, it seemed even easier to concede the quality of aping. To continue our system, the gorillas would merely have to imitate certain attitudes and deliver a few harangues, all based on the same model.

I thus came to view the most diverse activities of

our Earth with a new eye and to imagine them performed by apes. I indulged with a certain satisfaction in this game, which demanded no intellectual
effort. I called to mind a number of political meetings I had attended as a journalist. I remembered
the stock remarks made by the personalities I had
had to interview. I recalled with particular intensity
a celebrated trial I had followed several years
before.

The defense counsel was one of the masters of his
profession. Why did he appear to me now in the
guise of a proud gorilla, as did also the advocate
general, another celebrity? Why did I compare their
gestures and actions to conditioned reflexes resulting
from intensive training? Why did the president of the
tribunal remind me of a solemn orangutan reciting
sentences learned by heart, the utterance of which
was automatic and likewise inspired by some state-
ment from a witness or some murmur in the crowd?

I thus spent the last part of the journey obsessed
by comparisons that seemed to me significant. When
I came to the world of finance and business, my
final mental picture was a thoroughly simian vision,
a recent recollection of the planet Soror. It was
during a visit to the stock exchange, where my
friend Cornelius had insisted on bringing me, for it
was one of the curiosities of the capital. This is
what I saw—a picture I recalled with extraordinary
vividness during the last minutes of my flight.

The stock exchange was a large building, outwardly imbued with a strange atmosphere created by a vague buzz of voices that grew progressively louder as one approached, until it was a deafening roar. We went inside and were forthwith caught up in the turmoil. I wedged myself against a pillar. I was accustomed to individual apes but was always somewhat stupefied when surrounded by a compact mob, as now. I found the sight even more incongruous than that of the learned assembly during the famous congress. Imagine a hall of vast proportions crammed full of apes, screaming, gesticulating, and running hither and thither in a completely disorganized manner, apes in hysteria, apes who not only rushed about and bumped into one another on the floor but who formed a swarming mass right up to the ceiling, which was at a giddy height from the ground. The place was equipped with ladders, trapezes, and ropes that they used constantly in order to move from one spot to another. They thus filled the entire volume of the building, which assumed the aspect of a cage specially designed for a grotesque exhibition of fourhanded creatures.

The apes literally flew to and fro across this space, always catching hold of some piece of equipment just when I thought they were about to fall; all this in a hubbub of infernal exclamations, shouts, cries, and even sounds that recalled no civilized language. They were monkeys there who were *barking*—

yes, barking for no apparent reason—swinging themselves from one end of the room to the other on long ropes.

"Have you ever seen anything like it?" my friend Cornelius asked me proudly.

I readily admitted I had not. It needed all my previous acquaintance with the apes to convince me that these were rational creatures. No one in his right mind who watched this circus could escape the conclusion that he was witnessing the frolics of madmen or animals gone wild. Not a glimmer of intelligence could be seen in their eyes, and they all looked alike. I could not tell one from another. All of them were dressed in the same way and wore the same mask, which was the mask of madness.

The most disturbing part of my present image was that, contrary to the phenomenon that shortly before had made me assign the form of gorillas or orangutans to the figures in the earthly scene, I now saw the members of this insane crowd in the guise of human beings. It was men I thus saw shrieking, barking, and swinging about on ropes to reach their destination as fast as possible. In excitement I recalled other aspects of this scene. I remembered that after looking on for some time, I had begun to notice certain details suggesting vaguely that this hubbub did nevertheless form part of a civilized system. An articulate word could occasionally be heard above the bestial shrieks. Perched on a scaffolding at a giddy height above us, a gorilla, without interrupting the hysterical gestures of his hands, would pick up a piece of chalk in his foot and write some probably significant figure on a blackboard. To this gorilla, too, I assigned human features.

I managed to rid myself of this hallucination only by coming back to my rough outline of a theory on the origins of the simian civilization, and in this remembrance of the world of finance I found fresh arguments to support it.

The aircraft touched down. I was back in the capital. Zira had come to meet me at the airport. From far off I saw her scarf pulled down over her ears, and the sight of it filled me with joy. When I eventually joined her after the customs formalities I had to restrain myself from flinging my arms around her.

thirty-one

I spent the month following my return in bed, suffering from an infection I had probably picked up on the site and which assumed the form of violent bouts of fever similar to malaria. I was not in pain, but my brain was on fire and I could not stop mulling over the elements of the fearful truth I had glimpsed. There was no longer any doubt in my mind that a human era had preceded the simian age on the planet Soror, and this conviction gave me a sort of intoxication.

On second thought, however, I am not sure if I ought to feel proud of this discovery or profoundly humiliated by it. My self-respect notes with satisfaction that apes have invented nothing, that they are mere imitators. My humiliation derives from the fact that a human civilization could have been so easily assimilated by apes.

How could this have happened? In my delirium I could not keep my mind off the problem. True, we have long known that our civilizations are mortal, but such a complete disappearance makes the senses reel. A sudden disaster? A cataclysm? Or else the slow decline of the one and the progressive ascent of the other? I am inclined to the latter hypothesis, and I find extremely significant indications of this evolution in the apes' present-day condition and preoccupations.

The importance they attach to biological research, for instance—well, I am fully aware of its origin. In the old days many apes must have served as experimental subjects for men, as is the case in our own laboratories. These were the ones who first hoisted the flag, who were the pioneers of the revolution. They would naturally have begun by imitating the gestures and attitudes observed in their masters, and these masters were researchers, learned biologists, doctors, nurses, and warders. Hence this unusual imprint on most of their enterprises, which still persists today.

And what about the men all this time?—enough speculation about apes!

It is now two months since I visited my former companions in captivity, my fellow humans. Today I feel better. I have no more fever. Yesterday I told Zira—Zira has looked after me like a sister during my illness—I told her that I was planning to resume my work in her department. She did not seem very pleased but she raised no objection. It is time for me to pay my visit.

Here I am again in the room with the cages. A strange emotion makes me pause on the threshold. I now see these creatures in a new light. It is with anguish that I wonder, before making up my mind to enter, if they will recognize me after my long absence. Well, they do recognize me. All their eyes are fixed on me, as they always used to be, and even with a sort of deference. Am I dreaming or do I really discern a new look in them, a look reserved for me and different from the glances they bestow on their ape warders? A gleam impossible to describe, but in which I fancy I see an awakened curiosity, an unusual emotion, shades of ancestral memories trying to emerge from bestiality, and perhaps . . . an uncertain glimmer of hope.

This hope, I believe, I have myself unconsciously nourished for some time. Is it not the reason why I am overwhelmed by this feverish excitement? Is it not I, I, Ulysse Mérou, the man whom destiny has brought to this planet to be the instrument of human regeneration?

Here, distinctly stated at last, is the hazy notion that has been haunting me for a month. The good Lord does not shoot dice, as a certain physicist once said. Nothing happens by mere chance in the cosmos. My voyage to the world of Betelgeuse was decreed by a superior consciousness. It is up to me to show myself worthy of the choice and to be the new savior of this human race in decline.

As before, I go slowly around the cages. I force myself not to rush over to Nova's cage at once. Is the envoy of destiny entitled to favorites? I speak to each of my subjects. The moment has not yet come for them to talk. I do not mind. I have my entire lifetime in which to accomplish my mission.

I now approach my former cage with studied negligence. I look out of the corner of my eye, but I do not see Nova's arms stretched through the bars, I do not hear the cries of joy with which she always used to greet me. A strange misgiving assails me. I cannot restrain myself. I dash forward. The cage is empty.

I summon one of the warders in an authoritative voice that makes the captives shiver. Zanam is the one who appears. He does not like receiving orders from me, but Zira has instructed him to put himself at my disposal.

"Where is Nova?"

He replies in a surly manner that he does not know. She was taken away one day without any reason being given. I repeat my question but in vain. At this moment, luckily, Zira turns up to carry out her tour of inspection. She sees me in front of the empty cage and realizes why I am so upset. She looks flustered and at once starts talking about something else.

"Cornelius has just come back. He wants to see you."

At the moment I don't give a damn about Cornelius or the chimpanzees or the gorillas or any other creature in heaven or in hell. I point at the cell with my finger.

"Where's Nova?"

"She's ill," says Zira. "She's been transferred to a special wing."

She beckons to me and leads me aside, out of earshot of the warder.

"The administrator made me promise to keep it secret. But I feel you ought to know."

"She's ill?"

"Nothing serious; but it's important enough to put the authorities on their toes. Nova is expecting."

"She's . . ."

"I mean she's pregnant," the she-ape announces, observing me with a curious expression.

thirty-two

I am stupefied without yet fully realizing what this news implies. At first I am assailed by a mass of trivial details and above all tormented by the disquieting question: why was I not notified of this? Zira does not give me time to protest.

"I noticed two months ago, on my return from the trip. The gorillas had not seen a thing. I phoned Cornelius, who had a long conversation with the administrator. They agreed that it would be better to keep it secret. No one knows about it except them and me. She's in an isolated cage and I'm looking after her personally."

I regard this concealment as an act of treachery on Cornelius' part and I can see that Zira is embarrassed. It looks to me as though some plot is being hatched in the background.

"Don't worry. She is being well treated and there's nothing she needs. I'm doing everything I can for her. No pregnancy of a female human has ever been so carefully watched over."

Under her mocking gaze I lower my eyes like a schoolboy guilty of some misdemeanor. She makes an effort to assume an ironical tone, but I can see she is perturbed. True, I realize my physical intimacy with Nova has vexed her ever since she recognized my true nature, but there is more than vexation in her expression. It is her affection for me that makes her anxious. These mysteries concerning Nova presage nothing good. I imagine she has not told me the whole truth: that the Grand Council is well aware of the situation and there have been discussions at a very high level.

"When is her confinement due?"

"In three or four months."

The tragi-comic side of the situation overwhelms me suddenly. I am about to become a father in the system of Betelgeuse. I am going to have a child on the planet Soror by a woman for whom I feel a great physical attraction and sometimes even compassion but who has the mind of an animal. No other being in the cosmos has found himself involved in such an adventure. I feel like weeping and laughing at the same time.

"Zira, I want to see her!"

She gives a little pout of annoyance.

"I knew you would ask me that. I've already discussed it with Cornelius and I think he will agree to it. He's waiting for you in his office."

"Cornelius is a traitor!"

"You've no right to say that. He is divided between his passion for science and his duty as an ape. It is only natural that he should feel extremely apprehensive at this impending birth."

My anguish increases as I follow her down the corridors of the institute. I can imagine the attitude of the learned apes and their fear of seeing a new race arise that—Good heavens! I now see exactly how the mission with which I have been entrusted can be accomplished.

Cornelius greets me in a friendly manner, but a permanent awkwardness has been created between us. At times he looks at me as though in terror. I make an effort not to broach the subject on my mind at once. I ask him about the voyage and the end of his stay among the ruins.

"Fascinating. I have a mass of irrefutable proof."

His clever little eyes are sparkling. He cannot prevent himself from exulting over his success. Zira is right; he is torn between his love of science and his duty as an ape. At the moment it is the scientist speaking, the enthusiastic scientist for whom only the triumph of his theories counts.

"Skeletons," he says. "Not one, but a whole collection, discovered in such order and circumstances as to make it incontestably clear that we had come upon a graveyard. Enough evidence to convince the most obtuse mind. Our orangutans, of course, insist on regarding it as a mere coincidence."

"What about these skeletons?"

"They are not simian."

"I see."

We look each other straight in the eye. With his enthusiasm somewhat diminished, he slowly continues, "I can't hide it from you; you've already guessed. They are the skeletons of men."

Zira is certainly in the know, for she shows no surprise. Both of them again observe me closely. Cornelius finally makes up his mind to discuss the matter frankly.

"I am now certain," he admits, "that there once existed on our planet a race of human beings endowed with a mind comparable to yours and to that of the men who populate your Earth, a race that has degenerated and reverted to an animal state. . . . Furthermore, since my return here I have been given additional evidence to support this hypothesis."

"Additional evidence?"

"Yes. It was discovered by the director of the encephalic section, a young chimpanzee with a great future. He may even be a genius. . . . You would be wrong to think," he continued with heavy sarcasm, "that apes have always been imitators. We have made some remarkable innovations in certain branches of science, especially in connection with these experiments on the brain. I'll show you the results some day, if I can. I'm sure you'll be amazed by them."

He seems anxious to convince himself and expresses himself with unusual aggressiveness. I have never attacked him on this point. He was the one who first mentioned the lack of creative faculty in apes, two months ago. In a boastful tone he continues:

"Believe me, the day will come when we shall surpass men in every field. It is not just by accident, as you might imagine, that we have managed to succeed them. This result was foreordained in the normal course of evolution. Rational man having had his day, a superior being was bound to succeed him, preserve the essential results of his conquests, and assimilate them during a period of apparent stagnation before soaring up to even greater heights."

This is a new way of visualizing the outcome. I might well retort that many men on Earth have had the presentiment of a superior being who may one day succeed them but that no scientist, philosopher, or poet has ever imagined this super-human in the guise of an ape. But I do not feel inclined to pursue the point. The essential, after all, is that the mind should embody itself in some organism. The form of the latter is of little importance. I have many other more pressing subjects. I bring the conversation around to Nova and her condition. He makes no comment and tries to console me.

"Don't worry. It will be all right, I hope. It will

probably be a child like any other human child on Soror."

"I certainly hope not. I'm convinced it will talk!"

I cannot help protesting indignantly. Zira gives a frown to make me keep quiet.

"Don't be too hopeful," Cornelius solemnly says, "for her sake and for your own."

He adds in a friendlier tone, "If he talked, I don't know if I should be able to go on protecting you as I do. Don't you realize that the Grand Council is on tenterhooks and that I've been given the strictest orders to keep this birth a secret? If the authorities discovered you knew all about it, I should be dismissed, so would Zira, and you'd find yourself alone among . . ."

"Among enemies?"

He turns his head away. That is exactly what I thought: I am regarded as a danger to the simian race. Nevertheless, I am happy to feel I have an ally in Cornelius, if not a friend. Zira must have pleaded my cause more fervently than she gave me to understand and he will do nothing that might displease her. He gives me permission to go and see Nova—in secret, of course.

Zira leads me to an isolated little building to which she alone holds the key. The room into which she shows me is not very big. It contains only three cages, two of which are empty. Nova occupies the third. She has heard us coming and her instinct has warned her of my presence, for she has risen to her feet and stretched out her arms even before seeing me. I clasp her hands and rub my face against hers. Zira gives a contemptuous shrug, but she hands me the key of the cage and goes to keep watch outside in the corridor. What a good soul this she-ape is! What woman would have been capable of such tact? She knows we must have a lot of things to say to each other and therefore leaves us to ourselves.

A lot of things to say? Alas! I have again forgotten Nova's miserable condition. I rush into the cage and fling my arms around her. I speak to her as though she is able to understand—as I might speak to Zira, for instance.

Does she not understand? Does she not have at least a vague intuition of the mission for which both of us are responsible from now on, she as well as I?

I lie down on the straw by her side. I stroke the incipient fruit of our outlandish passion. It seems to me nonetheless that her present condition has given her a personality and dignity she did not have before. She trembles as I pass my fingers over her stomach. Her eyes have certainly acquired a new intensity. Suddenly, with a great effort, she stammers out the syllables of my name, which I have taught her to articulate. She has not forgotten her lessons. I am overwhelmed with joy. But her eye dulls again and she turns aside to devour the fruit I have brought her.

Zira comes back; it is time to say good-by. I leave with her. Sensing my feeling of loss, she accompanies me back to my apartment where I burst into tears like a child.

"Oh Zira, Zira!"

While she cradles me in her arms like a mother, I begin to speak to her, to speak to her with affection, without stopping, relieving myself at last of the surfeit of emotions and thoughts that Nova is unable to appreciate.

thirty-three

Admirable she-ape! Thanks to her, I was able to see Nova fairly often during this period, without the authorities knowing. I spent hours on the lookout for the intermittent gleam in her eye, and the weeks went by in impatient expectancy of the birth.

One day Cornelius decided to take me to the encephalic section, the wonders of which he had described to me. He introduced me to the head of the department, the young chimpanzee called Helius, whose genius he had praised to the skies, and apologized for not being able to show me around himself because of some urgent work.

"I'll come back in an hour's time to show you the pearl of these experiments myself," he said, "the one that affords the evidence I told you about.

Meanwhile I'm sure you'll be interested in the classic cases."

Helius showed me into a room similar to those in the institute, equipped with two rows of cages. On entering, I was struck by a pharmaceutical smell reminiscent of chloroform. It was indeed an anesthetic. All the surgical operations, my guide informed me, were now performed on subjects who had been put to sleep. He stressed this point, as though to show the high degree attained by simian civilization, which was at pains to suppress all useless suffering, even in men. I could thus be reassured.

I was only half reassured. I was still less so when he ended by mentioning an exception to this rule: the very experiments, in fact, whose aim is to make a study of pain and localize the nerve centers from which it derives. But I was not to see any of these today.

This was not calculated to appease my human sensibility. I remembered that Zira had tried to dissuade me from visiting this section, where she herself came only when she had to. I felt like turning around and retracing my steps, but Helius did not give me time to do so.

"If you would like to attend an operation, you will see for yourself that the patient suffers no pain at all. No? Well, let's go and see the results then."

Passing by the closed cell from which the smell emanated, he led me toward the cages. In the first I saw a young man of fairly handsome appearance but extreme emaciation. He was propped up on a litter. In front of him, almost under his nose, stood a bowl containing a mash of sweetened cereals to which all men were partial. He was gazing at it in bewilderment without making the slightest gesture.

"You see," said the director. "This boy is famished, he has not eaten for twenty-four hours. Yet he does not react when confronted with his favorite food. This is the result of partial ablation of the frontal brain, which was performed on him some months ago. Since then he has been continuously in this state and has to be fed by force. You can see how thin he is."

He signaled to a nurse, who went into the cage and plunged the young man's face into the basin. The latter than began lapping up the mash.

"A fairly commonplace case. Here are some more interesting ones. On each of these subjects we've performed an operation affecting various areas of the cerebral tissue."

We walked past a series of cages occupied by men and women of all ages. At the door of each of these was a panel specifying the operation performed, with a wealth of technical details.

"Some of these areas are related to the natural reflexes; others to the acquired reflexes. This one, for instance—"

This one, according to the case history, had had a whole zone of the occipital area removed. He could no longer distinguish the distance or shape of objects, a disability he manifested by a series of disorganized gestures whenever a nurse approached him. He was incapable of avoiding a stick placed in his path. On the other hand, a piece of fruit held out to him inspired him with alarm and he tried to draw away from it in terror. He could not grasp the bars of his cage and made grotesque attempts to do so, closing his fingers on empty air.

"This other one here," said the director with a wink, "was once a remarkable subject. We had succeeded in training him to an astonishing degree. He answered to his name and, to a certain extent, obeyed simple orders. He had solved fairly complicated problems and learned how to use rudimentary tools. Today he has forgotten all his education. He does not know his name. He cannot perform the slightest trick. He has become the stupidest of all our men—as a result of a particularly difficult operation: extraction of the temporal lobules."

With my stomach heaving at this succession of horrors accompanied by comments from a grinning chimpanzee, I saw men partially or totally paralyzed, others artificially deprived of sight. I saw a young mother whose maternal instinct—once highly developed, so Helius assured me—had completely disappeared after interference with the cervical cortex. She kept pushing away her young child whenever it attempted to approach her. This was too much for me. I thought of Nova, of her impending motherhood, and clenched my fists with rage. Luckily Helius showed me into another room, which gave me time to recover my composure.

"Here," he said with a mysterious air, "we indulge in more delicate research. It's no longer the scalpel that is brought to bear, it's a far more subtle medium—electrical stimulation of certain spots of the brain. We have brought off some remarkable experiments. Do you practice this sort of thing on Earth?"

"Yes, on apes!" I retorted in fury.

The chimpanzee kept his temper and smiled.

"Of course. However, I don't think you could ever have obtained such perfect results as ours, comparable to those that Dr. Cornelius wishes to show you himself. Meanwhile let's continue with our rounds of the commonplace cases."

He again led me up to some cages where nurses were in the process of operating. The subjects here were stretched out on a sort of table. An incision in the skull laid bare a certain area of the brain. One ape was applying the electrodes while another was attending to the anesthetic.

"You will note that here, too, we put the subjects to sleep: a mild anesthetic, otherwise the results would be falsified, but the patient feels no pain."

Depending on the point at which the electrodes were applied, the subject made various movements, usually affecting only one side of his body. One man jerked his leg up at each electric shock, then stretched it out again as soon as the current was

switched off. Another performed the same movement with one arm. In the next case it was the
whole shoulder that began twitching spasmodically
under the effect of the current. Farther on, with a
very young patient, it was the area commanding the
jaw muscles that was brought into play. The poor
wretch started champing, endlessly champing, with
a ghastly grin on his face, while the rest of his adolescent body remained motionless.

"Now look what happens when the duration of
the contact is increased," said Helius. "Here is an
experiment carried to its utmost limit."

The creature on which this treatment was im-
posed was a lovely young girl who in certain respects reminded me of Nova. Several nurses, male
and female apes in white smocks, were buzzing
about her naked body. The electrodes were fixed by
a she-ape to the young girl's face. The girl at once
started moving the fingers of her left hand. The she-
ape kept the current on instead of switching it off
after a few seconds, as in the other cases. Then the
movements of the fingers became frenzied and
gradually the wrist started twitching. A moment
later it was the forearm, then the upper arm and
shoulder. The twitching presently spread, on the
one hand to the hip, the thigh, and the leg all the way
down to the toes, on the other to the muscles of the
face. After ten minutes the whole of the wretched
girl's left side was shaken by convulsive spasms, a

dreadful sight, growing more and more rapid and more and more violent.

"That's the phenomenon of *extension*," Helius calmly observed. "It's well known and culminates in a state of convulsions presenting all the symptoms of epilepsy—an extremely strange epilepsy, moreover, affecting only one side of the body."

"Stop it!"

I had not been able to stifle the cry that rose to my lips. All the apes gave a start and turned toward me with reproving glances. Cornelius, who had just come in, gave me a friendly tap on the shoulder.

"I admit these experiments are rather bloodcurdling when you're not used to them. But you must bear in mind that thanks to them our medicine and surgery have made enormous progress in the last quarter of a century."

This argument did not convince me, any more than the memory I had of the same treatment applied to chimpanzees in a laboratory on Earth. Cornelius shrugged his shoulders and dragged me off toward a narrow passage leading to a smaller room.

"Here," he told me in a solemn tone, "you're going to see a marvelous achievement, which is absolutely new. Only three of us ever go into this room—Helius, who is personally in charge of this research and who has made such a success of it; myself; and a carefully selected assistant. He's a gorilla. He's dumb. He's devoted to me body and soul and, what is more, he's an utter brute. So you see the importance I attach to this work. I'm willing to show it to you because I know you'll be discreet. It's in your own interests."

thirty-four

I entered the room and at first could see nothing to justify this air of mystery. The equipment was the same as in the previous room: generators, transformers, electrodes. There were only two subjects, a man and a woman, lying strapped down on two parallel divans. As soon as we arrived they started observing us with a strange intensity.

The gorilla assistant welcomed us with an inarticulate grunt. Helius and he exchanged a few words in deaf-mute language. It was a far from commonplace experience to see a gorilla and a chimpanzee moving their fingers like this. I do not know why, but it seemed to me the height of absurdity and I almost burst out laughing.

"All is well. They are quite calm. We can begin a test right away."

"What sort of test?" I implored.

"I'd rather keep it as a surprise for you," Cornelius grinned.

The gorilla anesthetized the two patients, who presently fell asleep, and started up various machines. Helius went up to the man, carefully unrolled the bandage that covered his skull, and, aiming at a certain spot, applied the electrodes. The man remained absolutely still. I was questioning Cornelius with my eyes when the miracle happened.

The man began to talk. His voice echoed around the room with an abruptness that made me start, rising above the buzz of the generator. It was not an hallucination on my part. He was expressing himself in simian language, with the voice of a man from Earth or that of an ape on this planet.

The faces of the two scientists were a study in triumph. They looked at me with a mischievous glint in their eyes and reveled in my stupefaction. I was about to utter an exclamation, but they motioned me to keep quiet and listen. The man's words were incoherent and devoid of originality. He must have been captive in the institute for a long time and kept repeating snatches of sentences he had heard spoken by the nurses or the scientists. Cornelius presently put a stop to the experiment.

"We'll get nothing more out of this chap. But the main point is, he talks."

"It's amazing," I stammered.

"You haven't seen anything yet," said Helius. "He talks like a parrot or a gramophone. But I've done much better with her."

He indicated the woman, who was sleeping peacefully.

"Much better?"

"A thousand times better," said Cornelius, who showed the same excitement as his colleague. "Just listen. This woman also talks, as you'll soon hear. But she doesn't merely repeat the words she has heard in captivity. Her talk has an exceptional significance. By a combination of physico-chemical processes, of which I shall spare you the details, this genius Helius has succeeded in awakening in her not only her own individual memory but the memory of the species. Under electrical impulse her recollections go back to an extremely distant line of ancestors: atavistic memories reviving a past several thousands of years old. Do you realize what that means, Ulysse?"

I was so amazed by this extravagant claim that for a moment I really believed the learned Cornelius had gone mad; for madness exists among the apes, particularly among the intellectuals. But the other chimpanzee was already handling his electrodes and applying them to the woman's brain. The latter remained inert for some time, just like the man, then she heaved a deep sigh and started talking. She likewise expressed herself in simian language in a rather low but extremely distinct voice that changed from time to time, as though it belonged to a number of different persons. Every sentence she uttered has remained engraved on my memory.

"For some time," said the voice in a slightly anxious tone, "these apes, all these apes, have been ceaselessly multiplying, although it looked as though their species was bound to die out at a certain period. If this goes on, they will almost outnumber us . . . and that's not all. They are becoming arrogant. They look us straight in the eye. We have been wrong to tame them and to grant those whom we use as servants a certain amount of liberty. They are the most insolent of all. One day I was jostled in the street by a chimpanzee. As I raised my hand, he looked at me in such a menacing manner that I did not dare strike him.

"Anna, who works at the laboratory, tells me there have been a great many changes there as well. She dares not enter the cages alone any more. She says that at night a sort of whispering and chuckling can be heard. One of the gorillas makes fun of the boss behind his back and imitates his nervous tics."

The woman paused, heaved several anguished sighs, then went on:

"It's happened! One of them succeeded in talking. It's certain; I read about it in *Woman's Journal*. There's a photograph of him, too. He's a chimpanzee."

"A chimpanzee, the first! Just as I thought," Cornelius exclaimed.

"There are several others. The papers report fresh cases every day. Certain biologists regard this as a great scientific success. Don't they realize where it may lead? It appears that one of these chimpanzees has uttered some ugly threats. The first use they make of speech is to protest when they are given an order."

The woman fell silent again and resumed in a different voice, a somewhat pedantic man's voice:

"What is happening could have been foreseen. A cerebral laziness has taken hold of us. No more books; even detective novels have now become too great an intellectual effort. No more games; at the most a hand or two of cards. Even the childish motion picture does not tempt us any more. Meanwhile the apes are meditating in silence. Their brain is developing in solitary reflection . . . and they are talking. Oh! not very much, and to us hardly at all, apart from a few words of scornful refusal to the more intrepid men who still dare to give them orders. But at night, when we are not there, they exchange impressions and mutually instruct one another."

After a long silence a woman's voice continued, in anguish:

"I was too frightened. I could not go on living like this. I preferred to hand the place over to my gorilla. I left my own house.

"He had been with me for years and was a loyal servant. He started going out in the evening to attend meetings. He learned to talk. He refused to do any work. A month ago he ordered me to do the cooking and washing up. He began to use my plates and knives and forks. Last week he chased me out of my bedroom. I had to sleep in an armchair in the sitting room. Not daring to scold him or punish him, I tried to win him over by kindness. He laughed in my face and his demands increased. I was too miserable. I abdicated.

"I have taken refuge in a camp with other women who are in the same plight. There are some men here as well; most of them have no more courage than we have. It's a wretched life we lead outside the town. We feel ashamed and scarcely speak to one another. During the first few days I played a few games of patience. I haven't the energy any more."

The woman broke off again and a male voice took over:

"I had found, I believe, a cure for cancer. I wanted to put it to the test, like all my previous discoveries. I was careful, but not careful enough. For some time the apes have been reluctant to lend themselves to these experiments. Before going into Georges', the chimpanzee's, cage I had him held down by my two assistants. I got ready to give him the injection—the cancer-producing one. I had to give it to him in order to be able to cure him. Georges looked resigned. He did not move, but I saw his crafty eyes glance over my shoulder. I realized too late. The gorillas, the six gorillas I was holding in reserve for the infection, had escaped. A plot. They seized us. Georges directed the operation. He copied my movements exactly. He ordered us to be tied down on the table, and the gorillas promptly obeyed him. Then he picked up the hypodermic and injected all three of us with the deadly liquid. So now I have cancer. It's certain, for though there may be doubt as to the efficacy of the cure, the fatal serum has long since been tested and proved effective.

"After emptying the hypodermic, Georges gave me a friendly pat on the cheek, as I often did to my apes. I had always treated them well. From me they received more caresses than blows. A few days later, in the cage in which they had locked me up, I recognized the first symptoms of the disease. So had Georges, and I heard him tell the others that he was going to begin the cure. This gave me a new fright. What if it killed me off more quickly! I know I am condemned, but now I lack confidence in this new cure. During the night I succeeded in forcing the bars of my cage and escaping. I have taken refuge in the camp outside the town. I have two months to live. I am spending them playing patience and dozing."

Another feminine voice succeeded his:

"I was a lady animal tamer. I used to do an act with a dozen orangutans, magnificent beasts. Today

I'm inside the cage instead of them, together with some other circus performers.

"To give them their due, the apes treat us well and give us plenty to eat. They change the straw of our bedding when it becomes too dirty. They are not unkind; they punish only those of us who show reluctance and refuse to perform the tricks they have taken it into their heads to teach us. These are extremely advanced! I walk on all fours; I turn somersaults. So they are very good to me. I'm not unhappy. I have no more worries or responsibilities. Most of us are adapting ourselves to this regime."

This time the woman fell silent for a long time, during which Cornelius gazed at me with embarrassing insistence. I could read his thoughts only too well. Had it not been high time for such a feeble race of men, who gave in so easily, to make way for a nobler breed? I grew flushed and looked away. The woman continued in a more and more anguished tone:

"They now hold the whole town. There are only a few hundred of us left in this redoubt and our situation is precarious. We form the last human nucleus in the vicinity of the city, but the apes will not tolerate us at liberty so close to them. In the other camps some of the men have fled far off, into the jungle; the others have surrendered in order to get something to relieve their hunger. Here we have stayed put, mainly from laziness. We sleep; we are incapable of organizing ourselves for resistance. . . .

"This is what I feared. I can hear a barbaric din, something like a parody of a military band. . . . Help! It's they, it's the apes! They are surrounding us. They are led by enormous gorillas. They have taken our bugles, our drums and uniforms, our weapons, too, of course. . . . No, they haven't any weapons. Oh, what bitter humiliation, the final insult! Their army is upon us and all they are carrying are whips!"

thirty-five

Some of the results obtained by Helius have leaked out to the public. Probably it was the chimpanzee himself who could not keep his mouth shut in the enthusiasm of success. In the town they are saying that a scientist has succeeded in making men talk. Furthermore, the discoveries of the buried city are being discussed in the press, and although their significance is usually distorted, one or two journalists are close to suspecting the truth. As a result there is an uneasy atmosphere abroad, which is manifested by the increased wariness of the authorities about me, an attitude that is increasingly more disturbing.

Cornelius has many enemies. He dares not proclaim his discovery frankly. Even if he thought of doing so, his superiors would no doubt be against

it. The orangutan clan led by Zaius is in league
against him. They talk about a conspiracy against
the simian race and point me out more or less openly
as one of the factionists. The gorillas have not yet
adopted an official stand, but they are always against
anything that tends to disturb law and order.

Today I experienced a deep emotion. The long-
awaited event has taken place. First I was overwhelmed with joy but, on second thoughts, trembled
at the new danger it represents. Nova has given birth
to a boy.

I have a child, I have a son on the planet Soror. I
have seen him, but only with the greatest difficulty.
The security measures have become increasingly
strict and I was unable to visit Nova until the week
after the birth. It was Zira who brought me the
news. She at least will remain a true friend, whatever else may happen. She found me so perturbed
that she took the responsibility of arranging a
meeting for me with my new family. It was a few
days after the event that she took me to see them,
late at night, for the newborn child is under close
observation during the day.

I have seen him. He's a splendid baby. He was
lying on the straw like a new Christ, nuzzling
against his mother's breast. He looks like me, but he
also has Nova's beauty. The latter gave a menacing
growl when I pushed open the door. She, too, feels
uneasy. She rose up, her nails extended like claws,
but calmed down when she recognized me. I am

sure this birth has raised her a few degrees higher on the human scale. The fleeting gleam in her eye is now a permanent glow. I kiss my son with passion, without allowing myself to think of the clouds gathering over our heads.

He will be a man, a proper man, I'm sure. Intelligence sparkles in his features and in his eyes. I have revived the sacred flame. Thanks to me, a new human race is rising and will bloom on this planet. When he grows up he will be the first of the branch and then—

When he grows up! I shudder at the thought of the conditions of his childhood and of all the obstacles that will stand in his path. No matter! Between the three of us, we shall triumph, of that I am sure. I say the three of us, for Nova is now one of us. One need only see the way in which she looks at her child. Though she still licks him, in the manner of the mothers of this strange planet, her eyes radiate love.

I put him down again on the straw. I am reassured as to his nature. He does not talk yet, but—I am out of my mind, he is only three days old!—he will one day. Now he has started crying, crying like a human child and not whining. Nova hears the difference and observes him with awe and ecstasy.

It does not escape Zira's attention, either. She draws closer, her furry ears prick up, and she watches the baby for a long time, in silence, with a solemn expression. Then she signals me that it is time to go. It would be dangerous for all of us if I were to be found here. She promises to look after my son and I know she will keep her word. But I am also aware that she is suspected of being attached to me, and the possibility of her dismissal makes me tremble. I must not allow her to run this risk.

I embrace my family warmly and leave. Looking around, I see the she-ape likewise bend over this human body and gently put her muzzle to his brow before closing the cage. And Nova does not protest! She permits this caress, which must have become a daily occurrence. Remembering the antipathy she used to show toward Zira, I cannot help regarding this as a miracle.

We go out. I am trembling from head to foot and I see that Zira is as deeply moved as I am.

"Ulysse," she exclaims, wiping away a tear, "I sometimes feel this child is also mine!"

thirty-six

The periodic visits that I force myself to pay Professor Antelle are a more and more painful duty. He is still in the institute, but he has had to be moved from the fairly comfortable cell where I had arranged for him to be kept. He was pining away there and from time to time gave vent to outbursts of temper that made him dangerous. He attempted to bite his warders. So Cornelius then tried out another system. He had him put in an ordinary straw-lined cage and gave him a mate: the girl with whom he used to sleep in the zoo. The professor welcomed her noisily with an animal demonstration of joy, and immediately his manner changed. He has now taken a new lease on life.

It is in her company that I now find him. He

appears to be quite happy. He has put on weight and looks younger. I have done all I can to enter into communication with him. I try again today, but without success. He is interested only in the cakes I offer him. When the bag is empty he goes back and lies down beside his mate, who starts licking his face.

"Now you can see how intelligence can melt away just as it can be acquired," someone behind me mutters.

It is Cornelius. He is looking for me, but not to talk about the professor. There is something serious he wants to discuss. I follow him into his office, where Zira is waiting. Her eyes are red, as though she has been weeping. They seem to have bad news for me, but neither of them dares to speak.

"My son?"

"He's very well," Zira says abruptly.

"*Too* well," Cornelius mutters with a frown.

I know he is a splendid baby, but it is a month since I have seen him. The security measures have been tightened still more. Zira, who is suspect by the authorities, is under close surveillance.

"Much too well," Cornelius repeats. "He smiles. He cries like a baby ape . . . and he has begun to talk."

"At three months of age!"

"Baby words, but there's everything to indicate that he will talk properly later. In fact, he is miraculously precocious."

I am delighted. Zira is annoyed by my doting-father manner.

"But don't you realize this is a disaster? The others will never leave him in liberty."

"I know from a reliable source that some extremely important decisions are going to be taken about him by the Grand Council, which is to meet in two weeks' time," Cornelius remarks quietly.

"Important decisions?"

"Very important. There's no question of doing away with him . . . not for the moment, at least; but he'll be taken away from his mother."

"And I, wouldn't I be allowed to see him?"

"You least of all . . . no, don't interrupt me," the chimpanzee continues emphatically. "We didn't come here to feel sorry for ourselves but to work out a plan of action. Well, now I have some definite information. Your son is going to be placed in a sort of fortress under the surveillance of the orangutans. Yes, Zaius has been plotting for some time and he is going to get the better of us."

At this point Cornelius clenches his fists in rage and mutters some ugly oaths. Then he continues:

"Needless to say, the Council knows perfectly well how little that old fool's scientific views can be trusted, but they are pretending to believe he is more qualified than I am to study this exceptional subject, because the latter is regarded as a danger to our race. They are counting on Zaius to make it impossible for him to do any harm."

I am dumfounded. It is not possible to leave my son in the hands of that dangerous imbecile. But Cornelius has not yet finished.

"It's not only the child that is menaced."

I remain speechless and look at Zira, who hangs her head.

"The orangutans hate you because you are the living proof of their scientific aberrations, and the gorillas consider you too dangerous to be allowed at liberty much longer. They are frightened you might found a new race on this planet. But apart from this eventuality, they are frightened that your mere example might sow unrest among the men. Unusual nervousness has been reported among the ones with whom you are dealing."

This is true. In the course of my last visit to the room with the cages, I noticed a marked change among the men. It was as though some mysterious instinct had notified them of the miraculous birth. They had greeted my appearance with a concert of howls.

"To tell the truth," Cornelius abruptly concludes, "I'm very much afraid that within the next two weeks the Council might decide to eliminate you . . . or at least remove part of your brain on the pretext of some experiment. As for Nova, I believe it will be decided to put her out of the way as well, because she has been in such close contact with you."

It's not possible! I who believed myself entrusted with a semi-divine mission! I feel I am once again the most wretched creature living and give way to the most dreadful despair. Zira puts her hand on my shoulder.

"Cornelius is quite right not to have concealed anything from you. But what he has not told you is that we will not abandon you. We have decided to save all three of you, and we'll be helped by a small group of brave chimpanzees."

"What can I do, the only member of my species?"

"You must get away. You must leave this planet, to which you should never have come. You must go back where you belong, to Earth. Your son's safety and your own demand it."

Her voice breaks as though she is on the verge of tears. She is even more attached to me than I thought. I am also deeply upset, no less at her sorrow than at the prospect of leaving her forever. But how to escape from this planet? Cornelius has a plan.

"It's true," he says. "I've promised Zira to help you escape, and so I shall, even if it means losing my job. I shall thus feel I have not evaded my duty as an ape. For if a danger threatens us, it will be averted by your return to Earth. . . . You once said, I believe, that your spacecraft was still intact and could take you home?"

"Without the slightest doubt. It contains enough fuel, oxygen, and supplies to take us to the edge of the universe. But how am I to reach it?"

"It's still orbiting around our planet. An astronomer friend of mine has tracked it down and knows every detail of its trajectory. As to the means of reaching it? Now listen. In exactly ten days' time we are going to launch an artificial satellite, manned by humans, of course, on whom we want to test the effect of certain rays. . . . No, don't interrupt! The number of passengers will be limited to three: one man, one woman, and one child."

I grasp his scheme in a flash and appreciate his ingenuity—but what obstacles!

"Some of the scientists responsible for this launching are friends of mine, and I have won them over to your cause. The satellite will be placed on the trajectory of your craft and will be navigable within certain limits. The human couple have been trained to carry out certain motions through conditioned reflexes. I think you'll be even more skillful than they are. . . . For this is our plan: you three will take the place of the passengers. That shouldn't be too difficult. As I said, I've already got the necessary accomplices: chimpanzees regard assassination with repugnance. The others won't even notice the trick that's played on them."

This indeed is more than likely. To most of the apes, a man is a man and nothing more. The differences between one individual and another do not strike them.

"I'll put you through an intensive course of

training during these ten days. Do you think you'll
be able to board your craft?"

It ought to be possible. But it's not the difficulties
and dangers I am thinking about at the moment. I
cannot shake off the melancholy that assailed me
just now at the thought of leaving the planet
Soror, Zira, and my fellows, yes, my fellow humans. Toward them I feel I am something of a de-
serter. Yet above all I must save my son and Nova.
But I shall come back. Yes, later, I swear it on the
heads of the captives in the cages, I shall come back
with trump cards in my hand.

I am so bewildered that I voice my thoughts
out loud.

Cornelius smiles.

"In four or five years of your time, your traveling
time, but in more than a thousand years as far as we
stay-at-homes are concerned. Don't forget that we,
too, have discovered relativity. In the meantime I've
discussed the risk with my chimpanzee friends and
we have decided to take it."

We leave one another after making arrangements
to meet on the following day. Zira goes out first.
Remaining behind with Cornelius for a moment, I
take the opportunity of thanking him with all my
heart. Inwardly I'm wondering why he is doing all
this for me. He reads my thoughts.

"Zira's the one you ought to thank," he says.
"It's to her you will owe your life. On my own, I
don't know if I should have gone to so much

trouble or taken so many risks. But she would never forgive me for being a party to murder . . . and anyway . . ."

He pauses. Zira is waiting for me in the corridor outside. He makes sure she cannot hear and quickly whispers:

"Anyway, for her as well as for me, it is better that you should vanish from this planet."

He closes the door after me as I leave the room. I am alone with Zira and we take a few steps along the corridor.

"Zira!"

I stop and take her in my arms. She is as upset as I am. I see a tear coursing down her muzzle while we stand locked in a tight embrace. Ah, what matter this horrid material exterior! It is her soul that communes with mine. I shut my eyes so as not to see her grotesque face, made uglier still by emotion. I feel her shapeless body tremble against mine. I force myself to rub my cheek against hers. We are about to kiss like lovers when she gives an instinctive start and thrusts me away violently.

While I stand there speechless, not knowing what attitude to adopt, she hides her head in her long hairy paws and this hideous she-ape bursts into tears and announces in despair:

"Oh, darling, it's impossible. It's a shame, but I can't, I can't. You are really too unattractive!"

thirty-seven

We have brought it off. I am once again traveling through space aboard the cosmic craft, rushing like a comet in the direction of the solar system at an ever-increasing speed.

I am not alone. With me are Nova and Sirius, the fruit of our interplanetary passion, who can say "papa," "mama" and many other words. Also on board are a couple of chickens and rabbits, and various seeds that the scientists put in the satellite to study the effects of radiation on organisms of very diverse kinds. All this will not be wasted.

Cornelius' plan was carried out to the letter. Our substitution for the selected trio was made without difficulty. The woman took Nova's place in the institute; the child will be handed over to Zaius. The latter will demonstrate that he cannot talk and is nothing but an animal. Then perhaps I will not longer be considered dangerous, and the man who has taken my place, who will also not talk, will be spared his life. It is unlikely that they will ever suspect the substitution. The orangutans, as I've said before, make no distinction between one man and another. Zaius will triumph. Cornelius will have a few worries perhaps, but all this will soon be forgotten. . . . What do I mean! It is forgotten already, for aeons have elapsed out there during the few months I have been shooting through space. As for me, my memories are rapidly receding, like the material body of the supergiant Betelgeuse, as the space-time increases between us: the monster has changed in size to a small balloon, then an orange. It is now no more than a minute bright spot in the galaxy. So is it with my Sororian thoughts.

It would be unreasonable of me to fret. I have succeeded in saving the beings who are dear to me. Whom do I miss over there? Zira? Yes, Zira. But the emotions that came to life between us had no name on Earth or in any other region of the cosmos. The separation was essential. She must have recovered her peace of mind, bringing up her baby chimpanzees after marrying Cornelius. Professor Antelle? To hell with the professor! I could no longer do anything for him, and he has apparently found a satisfactory solution to the problem of existence. Only I shudder occasionally when I think that had I been placed in the same environment as he was, and without Zira's presence, I, too, might have fallen equally low.

The boarding of our craft took place without a hitch. I was able to draw closer and closer to it by guiding the satellite, and to enter the compartment, which had been left wide open for the eventual return of our launch. Then the robots went into action and closed all the exits. We were on board. The equipment was intact and the electronic brain started carrying out all the operations for our departure. On the planet Soror our accomplices pretended that the satellite had been destroyed in flight after failing to be placed in orbit.

We have been traveling for more than a year and a half of our own time. We have reached almost the speed of light, crossed an immense space in a very short time, and have already embarked on the deceleration period that is to last another year. In our little universe I never get tired of admiring my new family.

Nova is bearing the voyage extremely well. She is becoming more and more rational. Her motherhood has transformed her. She spends hours doting on her son, who is proving to be a better teacher for her than I was. She articulates almost correctly the words he utters. She does not yet talk to me, but we have drawn up a code of gestures enabling us to understand each other. I feel as though I had lived with her always. As for Sirius, he is truly the pearl of the cosmos. He is a year and a half old. He walks, despite the heavy gravity, and babbles without stopping. I cannot wait to show him to the men on Earth.

What intense emotion I felt this morning when I noticed the sun beginning to assume perceptible dimension! It appears to us now like a billiard ball and is tinged with yellow. I point it out to Nova and Sirius. I explain the nature of this heavenly body, which is new to them, and they understand. Today Sirius talks fluently and Nova almost as well. She has been learning at the same time as he. Miracle of motherhood, miracle that I initiated! I was unable to raise all the men on Soror from their animal state, but my success in Nova's case is complete.

The sun is growing bigger every moment. I try to distinguish the planets through the telescope. I can find my bearings easily. I can see Jupiter, Saturn, Mars, and . . . the Earth, yes, here is the Earth!

Tears come into my eyes. Only someone who has lived more than a year on the planet of the apes could appreciate my emotion. . . . I know that after seven hundred years I shall find neither parents nor friends, but I can hardly wait to see proper men again.

Glued to the portholes, we watch Earth approaching. I no longer need the telescope to distinguish the continents. We are in orbit. We are revolving around my old planet. I can see Australia,

America, and then . . . yes, here is France. We all three embrace, sobbing.

We embark in the vessel's second launch. All the calculations have been made with a view to landing in my native country: not far from Paris, I hope.

We have entered the atmosphere. The retro-rockets come into action. Nova looks at me and smiles. She has learned how to smile and also how to weep. My son stretches his arms out and opens his eyes in wonder. Below us is Paris. The Eiffel Tower is still there.

I have taken over the controls and am navigating very accurately. A miracle of technique! After seven hundred years' absence I manage to land at Orly— it has not changed very much—at the end of the air-field fairly far from the airport buildings. They must have noticed me, so all I need do is wait. There seems to be no air traffic; could the airport be out of use? No, there goes a machine. It resembles in every respect the aircraft of my day and age!

A vehicle moves off from the buildings, heading in our direction. I switch off my rockets, a prey to an increasingly feverish excitement. What a story I shall have to tell my fellow humans! Perhaps they won't believe me at first, but I have proof. I have Nova, I have my son.

The vehicle approaches. It is a truck and a fairly old-fashioned model: four wheels and a combustion engine. I automatically register these details. I should have thought such vehicles had been relegated to museums long ago.

I also expected a somewhat more official reception. There are very few people here to greet me. Only two men, as far as I can see. But how stupid I am—of course they cannot know. But when they do know . . . !

Yes, there are two of them. I cannot see them distinctly because of the setting sun reflected on the windshield, an extremely dirty windshield. Just the driver and one passenger. The latter wears a uniform. He is an officer; I can see the glitter of his badges of rank. The commander of the airport, probably. The others will follow.

The truck stops fifty yards from us. I pick my son up in my arms and leave the launch. Nova follows us after a moment's hesitation. She looks frightened but she will soon get over it.

The driver gets out of the vehicle. He has his back turned to me. He is half concealed by the long grass growing in the space between us. He opens the door for the passenger to alight. I was not mistaken, he is an officer; a senior officer, as I now see from his badges of rank. He jumps down. He takes a few steps toward us, emerges from the grass, and at last appears in full view. Nova utters a scream, snatches my son from me, and rushes back with him to the launch, while I remain rooted to the spot, unable to move a muscle or utter a sound.

He is a gorilla.

thirty-eight

Phyllis and Jinn raised their heads from the manuscript over which they had been bending together
and looked at each other for some time without
saying a word.

"A likely story," said Jinn at last, forcing a smile
to his lips.

Phyllis remained wrapped in thought. Certain
parts of the story had moved her and seemed to contain a germ of truth. She said so to her companion.

"It just shows there are poets everywhere, in every
corner of the cosmos, and practical jokers, too."

She pondered over this, but was not so easily convinced as he was. However, she reluctantly agreed.

"You're right, Jinn. That's what I think. . . .
Rational men? Men endowed with a mind? Men

inspired by intelligence? No, that's not possible; there the author has gone too far. But it's a pity!"

"I quite agree," said Jinn. "Now it's time we started back."

He let out the sail, exposing it to the combined rays of the three suns. Then he began to manipulate the driving levers, using his four agile hands, while Phyllis, after dismissing a last shred of doubt with an energetic shake of her velvety ears, took out her compact and, in view of their return to port, touched up her dear little chimpanzee muzzle.